D0174765

I AM MARGARET MOORE

ALSO BY HANNAH CAPIN

GOLDEN BOYS BEWARE
(originally published as FOUL IS FAIR)

THE DEAD QUEENS CLUB

I AM MARGARET MOORE

HANNAH CAPIN

WEDNESDAY BOOKS
NEW YORK

This is a work of fiction. All of the characters, organizations, and events portrayed in this novel are either products of the author's imagination or are used fictitiously.

First published in the United States by Wednesday Books, an imprint of St. Martin's Publishing Group

I AM MARGARET MOORE. Copyright © 2022 by Hannah Capin. All rights reserved. Printed in the United States of America.
For information, address St. Martin's Publishing Group, 120 Broadway, New York, NY 10271.

www.wednesdaybooks.com

Interior design and flag illustrations by Devan Norman

The Library of Congress Cataloging-in-Publication Data is available upon request.

ISBN 978-1-250-23957-0 (hardcover)
ISBN 978-1-250-23958-7 (ebook)

Our books may be purchased in bulk for promotional, educational, or business use. Please contact your local bookseller or the Macmillan Corporate and Premium Sales Department at 1-800-221-7945, extension 5442, or by email at MacmillanSpecialMarkets@macmillan.com.

First Edition: 2022

10 9 8 7 6 5 4 3 2 1

FOR THE GIRLS WHO CHOOSE
AND THE GIRLS WHO CANNOT

PART I

NAIAD

THE SUMMER

IT IS SUMMER AGAIN and we are alive.

All year we are ordinary girls. We trudge through snowbanks under gray skies. We study trigonometry late into the night. We ride horses and play piano; we put on new dresses for the homecoming dance; we give good-night kisses on bright doorsteps while our mothers peek through the curtains.

We exist, all apart from each other, in our own small corners of the world.

But today it is summer again and we are a thousand times more than that.

Today we are back at Marshall Summer Naval School. All the black-and-white winter is gone and the whole world is bold and gleaming.

It is our very last summer. In six weeks, in August, we will fold our uniforms and pack them into suitcases. We will press our palms to the gold M at the top of the stairs one last time: for luck and for tradition. We will leave forever, like all the girls before us.

But today it is summer again and it is ours.

And we are alive.

THE GIRLS

FLOR IS THE FIRST of us to arrive.

I see her from where I sit, cradled in a sycamore branch that bends out over the lake. I am wrapped in green shade but she stalks through sunlight, a leather suitcase in each hand. Her walk belongs to a girl who owns the world: shoulders thrown back, but the shadow of a slouch to her hips. She has come in a dark Cadillac with two men who might be uncles or guards or both. If her father had his way, they would follow her all summer. But here, for once, she is not *the general's daughter.*

Here we are only Marshall girls. We live behind glass and gray wood on green lawns. The forest hems us to the shore of Lake Nanweshmot; the forest keeps us safe away from the world. Here they push us until we break and heal and break again. We are everything and everything is ours.

Nisreen is next. She comes in with a swarm of girls and boys on the airport bus. She holds her sister's hand, her sister who is here for her very first summer, nine years old and a Butterfly. Nisreen crouches down and sunbeams strike through the gaps in the trees. She speaks soft and patient until her sister nods and holds herself straighter. At last she takes the path to the deck, alone.

A girl runs out fast enough for her heels to hit the hem of her kilt. She does not slow down. They crash together, meteoric, and something deep within the earth shifts back to where it always should have been.

Flor, swept up in the moment. Nisreen, swept up in Flor's arms.

They spin and spin there in the hot of the sun. Then they are walking, their steps matched and easy, with Flor carrying the heaviest of Nisreen's bags.

Rose is last. Her mother's car lets her out on the sidewalk, and Rose already has her Victory Race notebook under her arm and a cap pulled down tight over her curls. She is ready for summer and for winning. Before she makes her way into the deck she stops and gazes out along the shore; at the sycamore with its low branch.

I want with all my heart to jump down and run for her the way Flor ran for Nisreen. The way I ran, last summer, for a boy from Naval One.

This summer I will not run for him.

Rose disappears behind the gray wood building. I know every step she takes: up to the office to get her keys and turn in all the real-world things we aren't allowed here; then to the end of the hall, the last room on the north side. Flor has already made one bed with perfect square corners. She will be across the hall, in the room I share with Nisreen. Rose will make up her bed and hang her uniforms and tack pictures to the crumbling corkboard: one of every Winston at Marshall, and one of our first Butterfly cabin.

One from last June, before we turned tan and sun-bleached. Flor and Nisreen, Rose and me, fingertips clutching into each other's arms. Laughing and right.

When they are unpacked they will come out to me, and we will be together again, and it will be our summer: this is what I hope with all my life.

I sit in the crook of our sycamore and I wait for them.

I need them back. We need us back.

Everything depends on it.

I AM MARGARET MOORE

THE REFUGE

THE MARSHALL SUMMER NAVAL School stands proud on the north shore of Lake Nanweshmot. It is brick buildings and green lawns caught between the dark of the forest and the lake's jewel-blue; it is the toll of bells and the roar of the cannon. It smells like mud and gunpowder.

All winter it is a boarding school for boys, and the summer-camp cabins wait patient under heavy snow. In May the snow melts and they fling the doors wide and brush out the spiders and open the windows and let the world in.

We come back every summer—we Marshall girls. First we are Butterflies: nine and homesick, ten and eleven and home in the cabins close down by the road. Then we are Dragonflies, hewn strong and self-reliant from our endless weeks sailing on the water or riding horses deep into the woods. We can dress a wound and swim fearless across the deepest place in the lake. We know the leaves of every tree and the letters on the code-flags snapping high above the Naval Building. We say *Ma'am, yes ma'am.*

After six summers we earn our place in Upper Camp, split into decks we will love more than the winter-places we would call home if we did not have our refuge here. We are third-class girls, then second, then first. Every summer there is more of Marshall in our blood, and every summer there is more of ours in Marshall.

The lake and the trees and the pale mist rising: they are our dominion.

Together we are the Marshall Regiment. All thousand of us, from the Butterflies to the first classmen. In the Regiment we are seven battalions, and in the Upper Girls' Battalion we are six decks with three dozen girls in each. Three dozen girls who would die for us, and we would die for them. It is a thing like finding our fate when we learn, two months before third-class summer, which deck will be our sisterhood.

We Deck Five girls live in Gambol Hall. It is the worst dorm: everyone says it, even the Deck Six girls who live downstairs. It is far away from everything; it faces the lake dead-on and swarms with mayflies. It is hot and stifling and made of wood instead of brick: it is not meant to last.

They are wrong. It is perfect and forbidden.

We share it with every girl who has ever been Deck Five. Their names carved into the heavy wood desks. Their gold M nailed at the top of the stairs. Their stories soaked into the walls.

We call it Neverland.

Here we thread orange scarves through our collars and pin gold nametags over our hearts. We march and march until we can stay in step even blindfolded; we stand, hair spun with evening light, and sing our Deck Five hymn. Here we run and carry cinderblocks and plan, all summer, for the very last day: for the Victory Race, when we will stand together or fall.

This summer we are first-class girls. Our ninth summer and our last.

We have won the Victory Race and worn it like laurels. We have lost. We have climbed down the leaf-hidden point on the shore to trade kisses in sunset light. We summon ghosts around the campfire: the Marshall dead who linger in the dusk. We can find the place on the drill-field where the ground springs hollow. We know all the whispered stories of the secrets deep beneath.

I don't believe the stories. The truth is simpler, I think, and crueler.

Last summer the secrets were mine.

THE SECRETS

THEY COME OUT INTO the summer.

They take the lakeshore path that curves toward the Naval Building, a wide sweep beyond our sycamore. I climb down and follow the shore to where they sit, lined up on the brick walk that breaks off the path and leads nowhere. There was a pier there once, Rose says. It got old and broken and they tore it down. But it has been this way, dead-ending over the water, since our very first summer when we trooped along the shore and the counselor said, *Nanweshmot. Who can tell me where that name comes from?*, and Rose raised her hand high and said, *It's Potawatomi. It means a place to rest.*

Every summer this spot has been ours.

They stare out toward the south shore. Sunlight shines blinding on their hair. My eyes fill up with tears at seeing them again. Rose, my best friend in all my life, chin following a scow across the lake, and she is thinking already of the Victory Race and what we will make of us this summer. Flor with her hair braided tight and her jaw set firm, looking the future in the eye. And Nisreen: dark-circled and dreaming from her flight halfway around the world, but always the deep-dropped anchor to hold us fast.

Last summer knit us together and wrenched us apart. We left without goodbyes.

I wait behind them until the heat dries the tears on my cheeks, so Flor won't say *Mar, already crying and it's barely summer.* My heart could burst with how much I love them.

I breathe in and the summer fills up my lungs. We are

here again. We have never left. August has stitched itself to June with nothing else between them.

I step out onto the crumbling bricks. Then I am sitting there with them, next to Rose, and her skin is hot against mine.

Nisreen lets her head fall onto Flor's shoulder. A smile spreads across her face, warming us brighter than the daylight ever could.

She says, *We're back.*

We are.

In this moment in the sun we are us four again.

THE LINEUP

THERE ARE MISSING GIRLS. We see it and no one says anything. No one but Rose, standing to the side as we shuffle into place for supper roll-call.

Rose is unit commander today, and the second classmen mumble, *It isn't fair. Rose Winston should be reg com.* They whisper eager to the little third classmen, full of proud hard-earned knowing: *Rose Winston can sail in no wind. She should be reg naval, at least.*

Rose is UC, and she stands with her arms folded behind

her back as we fall into place. She casts a glance at Flor and mutters, "Where the hell are all our girls?"

Flor shrugs, eyes straight ahead, but Nisreen looks back at me. She stands where a first classman should be: Katherine Abbott, from New York, who last summer ran a faster mile than any girl in camp. Katherine Abbott, who did not come back.

Every summer there are girls who give up. Homesick third classmen who came to Upper Camp without being Butterflies and Dragonflies first. Tired second classmen who want *one summer of freedom,* without oh-six-hundred reveille, as though a Marshall summer isn't the best freedom in the whole world. Those girls who choose the world outside—they were never Marshall girls. Folding square corners and marching all summer doesn't make us Marshall. Threading orange scarves through our collars doesn't make us Deck Five.

But Katherine Abbott was Marshall through and through. A Deck Five girl as much as her sister, the one who was a first classman our last Dragonfly summer. And Isa Villanueva, our best third-class rower last summer and never homesick for even one second: she was Deck Five, too.

They are gone, and a dozen others, their places filled in with more third classmen than Deck Five has ever seen. Deck Five is never half new girls, because we are the best deck at Marshall.

Deck Five never quits.

Deck Five never runs away, and leaves her girls, and keeps herself from them.

Rose says, and it shimmers down our even rows: *Where the hell are all our girls?*

Behind me there is a whisper, quiet enough I could think I dreamed it, but it is real. A third classman who has not won her place yet, and still she knows too much, and still she says:

It's because of last summer, isn't it?

It's because of Margaret Moore.

THE GUILT

I LET THEM DOWN last summer.

It happened in a blur I cannot quite remember.

No: that is wrong.

The truth is, I could, I think, if I let myself.

I remember the storm.

I remember Nisreen in the dark saying what I had kept secret and still she knew: *Tell us, Mar—who is the boy?*

I remember how the phone rang and rang. The phone

we share all summer, one for the whole deck: black plastic, hanging from the wall, and hard and shiny like a beetle's shell. The stupid phone that barely worked except when we didn't want it to, and then it did, ringing and ringing until a third classman grabbed it up and said, *Mar, it's for you.*

I remember the storm rolling in. Lightning, orange and blue. Thunder like heaven splitting open. And my father's car takes the dark tree-tunneled bends of East Shore Drive, piercing a path streaked with rain. And the waves crash and the sailboats strain at their tethers, and the floor is soaked through.

When it storms on Lake Nanweshmot it storms furious and bright: in the daytime we watch the rain come across the water, stirring up the surface, hazing the sky. At night it is the rush of wind and the raindrops diving murderous into the floor, and when we try to jam the windows shut they stick, swollen, and we slip on the wet, and by the time we get them closed the storm is over.

I remember the storm.

I remember running away.

THE HALL

AFTER SUPPER WE RUN free. Third classmen try on friends that don't fit yet, the same as their too-big boat shorts. Boys and girls sit close beneath the trees on the Admiral's Walk.

We wander up the hill to the gymnasium. The left-hand door is shut: it is bad luck to open it, and tradition to leave it closed, and we are Marshall girls. We file through the other door. Then we fan out again and walk the Hall of Honor, past portraits of every Winter School since 1896 and every Summer Naval School since 1899. Without the years we would not know the difference. The Marshall M stands wide and proud, the way it has forever. The boys wear the same fresh white.

We sink to a stop at the second-to-last portrait. "Look at us," says Nisreen, floating closer, and we do. Deck Five jostles our place at the center. We beam bright, with sun-tanned faces and our hair still wet.

"Deck Five the proud, Deck Five the bold," says Nisreen, soft.

We are there again, two summers ago, an hour before the portrait: Naval Band on the shore, trumpets flashing in the sun, playing the Navy fight song too fast. The whole camp singing, from the first classmen down to the Butterflies. Deck Five in the water and stinking like mud and shrieking, *We won, we won.*

The sun is August-hot. The Victory Race is ours. We are girls and we are unconquerable.

Nisreen says, four fingers against the glass, "I miss—"

"We'll be back," says Rose. "Deck Five, with all the banners."

There is a rustling and the weight of stares from down the hall. We look back to the doors. A half-dozen Deck Four girls hover close.

The end of last summer, whispers one of them, loud enough for us to hear. *The night before the Victory Race, and there was an awful storm.*

Rose doesn't move, but I can feel the curse under her breath.

Deck Five—it was a mutiny, says the Deck Four girl. *Margaret Moore got kicked out of camp, and she ran out into the storm when they came to find her, and her whole deck went after her—*

Her voice slips down so it is only a brush of air. The tension strains. Nisreen's hand moves to catch Flor's arm.

The Deck Four girl says, *They canceled the Victory Race—*

"They canceled it," says Flor, all at once and stepping out in front of me. "But who would've won if they didn't?"

They pause. From out on the lawn a breeze coils in and plays against their hair.

"Blame us all you want," says Flor. "It will never make you Deck Five."

She holds her ground until they blush and look away; until they mutter excuses and slip back out again.

"It will be like this," says Nisreen when the silence seeps in. "They'll come for us this summer."

Flor says, unyielding, "Let them."

They look to where I stand against our photograph. It is two summers old. Last summer they sent Deck Five away before they took the portrait.

Last summer it was my fault.

"They'll fight," says Rose. "We'll win. Come on, let's go—let's go down to the pier—"

They turn for the far doors and the light through the windows paints them angelic. Rose says, like we sang from the lake with the Navy hymn sounding, *Deck Five the proud, Deck Five the bold.*

They are swallowed up in heat and light. I should follow them, but I cannot leave us here—ourselves, our third-class summer, before I took the precious thing we had and broke it.

Rose says, and Flor with her, singing loud and unbeaten: *Our veins bleed orange, our hearts are gold.*

In the portrait, two rows behind us, there are the boys from Naval One with smiles that sear.

We're staunch and true and bright and brave, shout Flor and Rose. *Bound with our sisters 'til the grave—*

I look to my girls. Rose and Flor have slipped around the corner but Nisreen lingers.

I am afraid, the way I was last summer. We are here again and still I am afraid.

Come on, Rose calls, out under the sky. *Let's go.*

Nisreen says, soft and for me: *As Marshall girls we'll live and die. Forevermore we are Deck Five.*

I follow her out into the light.

The fear moves close behind me.

THE MANIFEST

THERE WAS ONCE A Marshall girl who lowered the flags with a storm rushing in from the west. Lightning came and shocked her all afire, and she fell charred and dead, and we do not know her name, and she is immortal: a statue with one hand outstretched beside the Legion Building.

There was once a Marshall boy who caught a fever. They sent him to the infirmary and told him to rest, to sweat out the sick in the room at the end of the hall. Night fell like a curtain and when the nurse came back he was stiff and dead, and we do not know his name, and he is immortal and hovering still in the corner of that room.

There was once a Marshall boy who flew far from the fold. The whole camp watched as he came up over the woods, but the plane was too hungry and there above the trees it took its last breath and crashed shrieking down onto the road. And we do not know his name, and he is immortal and made of new rules and new pavement where they filled the scar he left.

There was once a Marshall girl who coaxed her horse to jump too high. They fell in a flash of black and tan and red. The horse stumbled up, and charged round and round, and she lay still in the dust, and we do not know her name. And she is immortal and they say in the stables every June, to the Butterflies on their first day, *Sometimes it is wise to be afraid.*

THE REVEILLE

WE WAKE TO CANNON-FIRE.

Reveille is oh-six-hundred hours: the cannon shouting on the shore and the metal bell clanging. A second classman runs up and down the hall, ringing and ringing and yelling, *Wake up, Deck Five!*

Nisreen is awake and staring out the window at the glass-flat lake, one arm propped behind her head. The wall behind her is bare. Rose hangs a Marshall flag over her bed, whiter than the paint. Flor hangs the flag of Venezuela. *Yellow for riches, blue for the sea,* she told us our first summer, in our hot mosquito-bite cabin on the other side of the road. The flag hung behind the bunk she shared with Nisreen, bright in the cabin's shade. *Red for spilled blood.*

I sit up. The night's chill still holds the air. In the hall doors open and girls scuffle past, racing for the showers before the water turns ice-cold.

"Margaret," says Nisreen, without looking; with her gaze on the distant shore. "I missed you."

And the door flies open and cracks against her wardrobe. "Get up, lazy girl!" shouts Flor, and she is wrapped in a towel with her hair soaking wet, and she yanks back the wool blanket and the sheet, and she grabs Nisreen and pulls her out. They fall against the wardrobe and Flor kicks the door shut with one swift heel. Far off down the hall the counselor shouts, *No slamming doors.*

They kiss. Deep and true and wild, like I am not here at all, and Nisreen's nightgown is tangled, and Flor's hair drips water all over the tile. They come up breathless and bright. Nisreen's eyes steal to me. Flor laughs and says, "What? Were you telling Mar all our secrets?"

And she flips her hair at me and the water is cold and wonderful.

Breakfast roll-call is oh-six-thirty. Dress C's: our boat shorts and blue oxfords, our deck scarves, our saddle-shoes and crew socks and gold nametags. The girl who rang reveille has the bell again, darting through the hall as our doors slam shut, shouting, *One minute 'til lineup!*

We run for the stairs. One after the next our right hands reach up. One after the next we slap the gold M on the wall; we clatter downstairs; we fall into line for roll-call; we march to the mess.

When the boys march in I will not look for him.

We are early, and the sunlight warms the air and sifts through the leaves. High up in the tree next to our lines, there is a snarling angry buzz.

The naval companies call attention, one after another, cacophonous, beyond their barracks.

I will not look for him.

Naval One bursts into view at a quick showy clip. They halt at the steps to the mess, just in front of us.

I will not look for him.

There is a white-hot silence in the sunlight, like time has hitched to a halt. It comes again: the buzzing, louder and furious. And all at once something falls from the tree and lands with a thud on the mulch. It storms and wrestles. It is two big summer bugs fighting each other, I think: spinning and digging at the mulch, and buzzing fierce and desperate. In the second row a third classman turns her head to look, and Rose calls, "Eyes front."

My eyes are front, not looking as the buzzing whines higher. My eyes are front, where the Naval One UC salutes. His eyes are on the reg com, and then he does a sharp left face and his eyes are on his boys.

For one instant between, his eyes are on Deck Five.

He has found me.

THE BOY

I LOVED A BOY once, before all this. I loved him so strong and so true I can feel it still, like a knife to my stomach. So that every night when I closed my eyes his name was the last word still tracing its bright-lit path across the bleeding dark of sleep, and every morning it was the first thing to sift through with the sunlight.

His name was—

Nothing.

Nothing.

Nothing.

THE FALLEN

AFTER BREAKFAST I WALK out to the tree where we stood to wait for the boys. Beneath it there is a shiny thing that lies on its back. It is almost dead or dead already, one leg twitching.

It isn't two winged things, the way I thought. It is one: a fat cicada, black and wet, with half its body poking through a clouded shell. It tried and failed to molt from its old skin. And it buzzed and strained and fell to earth.

I pluck a single buttercup from along the stone ledge, missed when the groundskeepers sheared the grass short. I kneel on the path and place the flower there beside the cicada.

I stand watch until its twitching leg goes still.

THE DAYS

THE SUMMER FINDS ITS rhythm.

We wake at reveille.

We line up outside Neverland for roll-call at oh-six-thirty.

We march to the mess for breakfast. We go to morning classes. We line up for roll-call at eleven hundred hours. We march to the mess for dinner. We go to afternoon classes. We practice and match in the afternoon: sailing and wherries out on the lake; tennis and track; basketball in the stifling-hot gym with our shouts echoing high. We line up for roll-call at seventeen hundred hours. We march to the mess for supper. Tuesdays and Thursdays, we drill on the field and feel it spring in the hollow corner, and we line up for Retreat with our flag held high. After, the band plays, and we crowd into the tunnel with them while the rest of camp is stuck outside. They are much too loud, and out-of-tune, and inside the stone arch the sound breaks our bones. And it is perfect, and we jump and shout, and then at the very end they play the Navy hymn and we find each other and sing, *Deck Five the proud, Deck Five the bold.*

That first Retreat I look across at Nisreen and she is crying. She brushes the tears away but still I see.

Our first weekend we don't get permit, but we have three golden hours of freedom in the afternoon. We steal away to the pier and unfold under the sun. Flor and Nisreen practice semaphores: Flor swings two red-and-yellow flags, and Nisreen crouches on the pier scribbling the letters down. When they practice with a scribe they will run messages from Rose's book: complicated and misspelled, so they can't shortcut by guessing. But today Flor sends without looking away. Every time she triple-clacks the flags together to end the message, Nisreen smiles secret at what the letters spell.

Rose and I lie in a long crew-boat. The boat is the same as the wherries we take out in rowing class, but four times as big: enough room for eight girls rowing in pairs, and the smallest third classman shouting out the stroke. Rose has her boat shorts rolled up and her socks folded neat next to her saddle-shoes. She has found a boy: a boy from Aviation, short and silly last summer but this summer standing tall; the boy who will do the flyby tonight at Parade. She has chattered about him all day but she will never speak to him. She will gaze from far away until he marches off-step or comes second in a sailing race. And then she will forget him and find a new boy; a better boy.

She has chattered about him but now she has gone quiet, reading an old paperback with the front cover curled in.

I ask her what she is reading and she uncurls the cover as she turns the page: *The Tragedy of Hamlet, Prince of Denmark.* Back home Rose is a theater girl, trimming curtains instead of sails. She marks the pages the same way she marks her Victory Race notebook: swift and sure. She is left-handed but she writes with her right, so the ink won't smudge.

The waves lull and lap. The semaphores clack. I close my eyes and the whole world is warm and orange.

Rose murmurs lines: "'There are more things in heaven and earth, Horatio, Than are dreamt of in your philosophy.'" There is the scratch of pen on paper. There is a slow and languid pause. Girls shriek on the shore.

Poetry is a strange holy mystery to me: beautiful and secret. But Rose unlocks it the same way she unlocks equations and the shifting angles of the wind. With Rose everything is a number. She tells us she will work for NASA someday, writing long strings of numbers that send astronauts into infinity.

I will write words instead, I think.

The pen scratches again. Flor shouts and Nisreen laughs.

"'Let us go in together, And still your fingers on your lips, I pray,'" says Rose, and Flor's footsteps clatter on the pier. "'The time is out of joint. O cursèd spite, That ever I was born to set it right!'"

The boat rocks and I open my eyes. Flor and Nisreen have climbed aboard. Flor sits cross-legged; Nisreen stands next to her, towering tall with one hand shading her eyes.

"It's the yacht club regatta," she says.

We sit up and look out over the bow. Halfway across the lake a dozen scows hover in their starting line.

"Is your father racing?" Flor asks.

Rose nods, tucking her pen into her book. From out on

the lake the starting horn blares. The sails pull tight and the boats push east.

"We'll have permit next week. We could go to Summers Rest," says Rose. "I'll race, and you can watch from the dock."

"Your house is too far to tell the boats apart," says Flor.

On permit weekends we line up for our slips and we spirit away into town or the cottages dotting the whole long shore of Lake Nanweshmot. Last summer and the summer before, we four never went the three-mile trek to Rose's lakehouse. We went to mine instead: a tunneled deep-green mile to a driveway that curves through the trees. The house kneels humble on limestone blocks, nested in ivy. There is the garage door, set into the stone, where my father stores the C-scow. There is the ramp down into the water. There is the sunporch, caged in glass and greenhouse-hot with every sunset. There are the letters painted on the plank that hangs below it: SHADY BLUFF.

Last summer and the summer before, we sat baking on the sunporch, drinking sweet-sour lemonade and painting calamine lotion on our poison ivy spots. We ran down the ramp, our feet pale with the ghosts of our crew socks. We plunged into the water and swam out and out until it deepened from warm to cold. We wandered sunstreaked through the house, lakewater footprints bleeding into the wood floor. We were right and whole.

"It will be different this summer," says Rose, for me.

We are thinking of it: of last summer and the summer before. And I am thinking of the summer I was four years old, on the pier, and I stepped backward and fell flailing down into the clear green water. And my mother scoops me up and out, and I am about to cry and then I see her laughing and I am laughing too instead. The memory is fragile and blurred like I am seeing it all through that second I plunged in and looked up and the leaves were watercolors against the sky. My mother says, in the watercolor-blur, *Margaret! Little summer-girl. Never grow up, promise me? Promise you'll be my little summer-girl always.*

"Last summer—" says Nisreen.

"Don't," says Flor, but she takes Nisreen's hand when she says it. She never cries, not even our very first Butterfly summer when her uncle left her at the steps to our cabin. She is standing with a suitcase in each hand, and she is twenty-five hundred miles from home, and at home everything is uncertain. She is here to spend summer safe; to practice her English that is already perfect; to sharpen her discipline that could already cut stone. She is brave and calculating. She will stare at the girls who whimper and beg to go home. But her heart belongs to us, and to Nisreen, and she leaves it here in Neverland when the summer ends and picks it up again when we are back.

"I know," Nisreen says. She is gazing at the far-off branches that veil Shady Bluff. "But I don't."

"We know they tried to send Mar home," Flor says. The air-horn blasts once: the first scow has rounded the starting buoy. The second lap is on. "She ran out into the storm, and we chased after her, and they locked us up and sent us home—"

"We don't know anything," says Rose. "We don't know *why*."

They wait now, and I feel their eyes on me. I could say to them, *There was a boy*. But when I think of giving up his name, there is the fear that holds me by the neck: a fear that fades to gray and then to black beneath the storm.

It is my fault, I think. It is all my fault.

Nisreen still stares at the shore. "They sent us home when all we did was ask." She looks to me and looks away and says, "When we said there was a boy."

"They sent us home for no damn reason, you mean," says Rose.

Flor squints into the glare and gleam and says, "They had a reason. They kept it from us."

That is it: the place where all four of us stand in the dark, afraid of the answers and starving for them.

"We should find out the truth," says Nisreen. And if Flor is iron over a beating-soft heart, Nisreen is her perfect opposite. Tall but thin like a foal; a girl who lets the tears slip past her bristling lashes and catch the sunset at Retreat. She feels and feels. She gets sick every summer and spends nights in the infirmary with a rash eating at her ankles or white sores spotting her throat. But there is something in her that does not flinch: not from pain, not from love, not from truth. She will bend but never break. She will walk first into the dark.

The air-horn blasts twice: the second lap is done. Time has slipped by without us seeing.

"They owe us the truth," says Flor.

I think of that word, *owe*, and its round mournful sound. Last summer, we did not say goodbye. Last summer ends with a bright bolt of lightning, and rain on the road, and loss and rage, and truth and lies. I am afraid and I do not want to leave.

It is summer again. The sky is alight and the air holds us close and the crew-boat is real. I feel it with all ten fingers: the warm wood, rough and smooth at once, and bleached by sun, and stained with sweat and lakewater.

We are whole again and together, but I have kept myself from them.

I want to fix the pieces that are broken. Like sewing cuts with thick black thread; lashing splints to broken bones, the way we learned in our survival class. But that first-aid is only temporary. To heal we will have to go and pull out the thorns stuck deep in our flesh.

I want to go back. The four of us, to Shady Bluff. I want it so much that I cannot find the words to say it. And I reach to nudge Rose's hand.

"Look at that! Would you look—" she cries out, and she is on her feet, and across the lake the wind has shifted all at once and knocked the first-place boat down, and the second boat sails past it swift and sure. It crosses the starting buoy and the air-horn sounds the victory.

Rose whirls to us, and the breeze throws her hair around her face. And she sees my hand reaching for where she sat, and she sees the question in my eyes, and she says, "Let's go back to Shady Bluff."

THE SILENCE

ON SATURDAY NIGHTS WE call home. Lining up in the hall, waiting for the phone. It is our only chance to talk to our parents and we have four minutes each. We forget the important things. We say, *No, I'm not tired* over stretching yawns.

We sit in line behind two third classmen who spent all the first week pestering, *please, just two minutes*, with the counselor shaking her head and telling them to write a letter, and the girls shrieking, *A LETTER?!*, like they will die of it.

"It's . . . how do we even know what's happened out there?" one of them says, second in line. "There could be a bomb big enough to wipe out New York City, and we wouldn't even *know*!"

"Yes," says Flor with her voice as flat as the wall. "And isn't it wonderful."

They are brand-new girls, the two in front of us. Girls from America—*Not America*, Flor would say, *the United States, where you are too safe to know you are safe.* Out across the world there are elections that will change everything; there are wars we have never heard of; there are girls who will learn in their four minutes that they will never go home. They will hear news like Flor heard one Lower Camp summer, the counselor calling her in.

"We really are in Neverland," says the other girl ahead of us.

"Shush," says Rose, who is UC even in her pajamas. "Think about what you're going to tell your parents."

She is away from the world, too. Her brother is a lieutenant in the Navy, on a ship on some far ocean, and late in the summer when we sit in the chapel and hear the long list of names ringing out in the Gold Star Ceremony there will be two Winstons there. Her brother is not in danger: that is what her father says. She worries still when she thinks no one is looking.

We wait in the line. We spend our four minutes and we hang up and hand the phone to the next girl.

When it is my turn, I don't call.

I am selfish, I think.

I could have a brother at sea, like Rose. I could have my country pushing and pulling, with my father right in the heart of it, like Flor. I could have all the complicated history, and the family on both sides, and the treaties and borders and uneasy peace, like Nisreen.

I have none of that. I have only last summer and the choice my parents made so I could not.

I am the luckiest girl in the world, I know it, and I am spoiled and selfish. But I cannot speak to them.

They have already spoken for me.

THE SHUTTERS

ON SUNDAY AFTERNOON ROSE and I go out on a boat she could manage alone. Flor and Nisreen have stolen off together and we sail away into the blue past the Lower

Camp woods; past the raft floating far out beyond the Naval Pier. It is the Island: the farthest point where we can go alone; where tradition says only first classmen can set foot; where first-class boys dare each other to moor their boats and jump into the lake without getting caught and gigged for breaking rules.

We should not sail past it, but Rose is a Winston, and we do. We press on until we have passed the bend where the shore falls back, and then Rose lets out the sail and we gaze into the cove.

Shady Bluff stands far off, hidden in the trees.

The boat isn't out. There is no glint of light off the sunporch windows. The winter shutters are closed tight.

It is June: it is almost July.

They should be here already. They are here already every summer: my mother driving out in May, opening up the windows and letting out the dead air of a winter spent asleep. Chasing off cobwebs and running the water until it flows clear. And my father, coming down every weekend to sail on the lake and sit in the shade reading books about men dead for two thousand years. He said, when I was packing for my first Marshall summer and worrying over six weeks with girls I didn't know, *Time is a funny thing, Margaret. These six weeks will be over before you know it. But this day is endless, too. Someday it will be your first-class summer—someday you'll be as old as your grandmother—and still this day will be so clear you'll swear no time has passed at all.*

He was right. I sit here in the boat with Rose, and still I feel the book he pressed into my hand: *The Roman Republic.* The sail flutters overhead, and still he is saying, *The things you do here will make you who you are meant to be.* I am staring out over the lake, and it is the same as it was that summer; as it was for my father when he was a Marshall boy.

It is the same. It is always the same. But this summer they have not come back.

I feel the questions Rose will not ask. She sees the answers I will not give.

We turn back for the north shore without a word.

THE FLAGS

IN THE EVENINGS WE practice code-flags and semaphores, begging out of one more round of athletics. By the second week they let us sit alone, and we burrow into the quiet in front of the Naval Building with *The International Code of Signals.*

On the water, two pairs of boys row wherries out to the

end of the pier and back, again and again. The ensign on duty is Rose's cousin, three years older, and he sits in the shade and doesn't shout when they go farther than they should.

"We need to practice the way it is in the Victory Race," says Rose as we hunch over a deck of cards with code-flags printed in yellow and red and blue. When we race an ensign will hoist the flags on the mast, and Rose will read out the letters. Last summer I was her scribe, paging quick through *The International Code of Signals* to find their meaning. By August we knew the book by heart.

"I'll be right back," says Rose, and she jogs for her cousin on the shore.

The evening is still and glowing. Out on the water the boys shout. Flor is fifty feet away, flinging semaphores high and sharp. Nisreen sits cross-legged, reading the letters to their second-class scribe: *Tango Echo Lima Lima break—*

"We're golden," calls Rose, coming back. She squares off at the third classman she has chosen to come after us: this summer she will learn to scribe, and next summer she will read. "I'm going up to the roof. I'll hoist the flags three at a time. Write them down. No mistakes."

She is running again, to the stairs up the side of the Naval Building. It looms squat but strong, prowed like a boat. On the flat roof, one line flies the American flag and the Marshall M, and another runs code-flags. Today they spell out *Delta Romeo Whiskey*, for Rose's cousin's initials.

Later in the summer, when the days blur into one unbroken sweep, they will spell things they shouldn't.

"There's no wind," says the third classman when the flags jolt down the mast.

"There might not be wind on Victory Race day," says the girl scribing for Nisreen. "Will you whine then, too?"

The first three flags make their way up. *Charlie Bravo Six: I require immediate assistance, I am on fire.* The third classman scribbles. Flor cracks the semaphores together and Nisreen says *break.* Rose lowers the flags.

"Deck Five!" a boy shouts.

He is here.

He is cutting across the field. He is smiling the way he was that very first night we walked the lakeshore path. The second classman scribing for Nisreen lets out a starry sigh.

He is here in front of me, a dozen steps away.

Rose's second hoist hangs listless on the mast: *Alfa Oscar Two.*

"Looks like you're ready to win the Victory Race again," he says.

"Yes—we are, yes. We'll be ready," says the second classman, stumbling over it.

"Hello!" Flor shouts. She clacks the semaphores together five times; eight. "Hello—" And she shouts something else, in Spanish, and the third classman beside me goes big-eyed even with her stare locked on the mast. The flags are lowering now, and out on the lake the wherry-boys yell back to the boy on the shore, jubilant and careless across the still water.

From the beach Rose's cousin calls, *sit down, boys—*

"You know," says the Naval One boy to the second-class girl. His hands are in his pockets, his thumbs tucked over the edge. He is easy and effortless and already the warm tan of August. He is a Marshall boy if there has ever been one, the way Rose is a Marshall girl. "We're supposed to cheer for our sister deck."

"Deck One won't win," says the stubborn third classman. She is still practicing, even with him standing there, even with the wherry boys splashing and sparring, even with Flor cursing up and down in Spanish and English and French, too.

"We're supposed to cheer for Deck One," says the boy. He won't look at me. He looks only at the second classman crouching at Nisreen's feet. "But I'll tell you a secret."

The second classman has forgotten all about semaphores. She is blinking bright eyes and parted lips. Sitting careful and on-purpose, her back arched and her neck curving, waiting breathless for whatever he will say.

I am here, last summer, on the lakeshore.

I am here, the summer before, with him.

There is a knife buried deep in my stomach and I think I will be sick.

"I've always loved Deck Five best," says the boy.

On the shore Rose's cousin shouts, *I'm serious, boys, I'm gigging Naval One—*

I jump up fast. There is a burst of breeze all at once, and the flags on the mast snap to attention. Their red and gold bleed to blazing orange.

He is looking at me. He sees me. We stand with nothing between us for the first time since that night in the storm. For one second everything is in his eyes, our whole ruined story, and his mouth drops open but no words come.

The breeze kicks high. There is the crash of waves where before there was only a glass-flat gleam, and Rose yells, and Flor yells, and Nisreen shrieks. On the water there is a great sharp cracking like bone against wood, and Rose's cousin is running for the pier.

I am running too, away and away, onto the lakeshore path, into the blinding orange of the sunset.

THE PAST

I LOVED A BOY once, before all this. I loved him so strong and so true that I looked for him everywhere: when the sail-boats were far out on the lake and he was bent at one tiller out of two dozen; when Naval One lined up for Retreat and he was one face in fifty, all in white and white; when we stood waiting to march into the mess and could not move even our eyes. I looked for him everywhere and I found him everywhere, and he looked for me and found me too.

His name was—

Nothing.

His name was nothing and so was mine. He was Naval One and I was Deck Five, and we were third classmen, and we were Marshall through and through. Naval One won their Valor Race and the next day Deck Five won Victory. He watched from the shore when we stood in the lake, triumph dripping down our backs.

He found me after, at the Last Night campfire, with Rose and Flor and Nisreen. S'mores stuck to our fingers and smoke steeped our hair. My face was tight with sunburn.

He said, *Will you walk with me?*

I said, *Yes.*

Why would I ever say anything else?

We walked away from the firelight, together. The brand-new gold pin on my collar poked at my skin. Later, back in Neverland when I undressed, I would find a patch of red where the pin had stuck me with every swing of my arm, and it would turn me proud.

We walked along the lakeshore path under too many stars to count. We walked through the veil of spider-threads spun across our way. My hand found the rough of the metal rail and his hand found mine.

He was beautiful and bright. He was summertime to last through cold Chicago winter. His hair was a deep brown that shone like polished wood and his eyes were as dark as the sky.

He kissed me there on the shore. My first kiss and my best. The waves hushed and I shut my eyes and when I opened them there were fireflies lighting up on the lawn, glowing orange, and it was magic and summer and a dozen little fires all our own.

He said, *I wish summer never had to end.*

THE MEETING

THEY CALL US TO the auditorium. It is late, almost taps, and the smallest Butterflies blink sleep out of their eyes.

I did not see it happen. But Nisreen saw, and Flor, and Rose high up on the roof, running for the railing with a red and blue flag clutched in her hand: *Echo.*

They saw the wherry-boys standing on their seats, swinging their oars, showing off for the boy on the shore. They saw the waves kick up just as one boy climbed bold onto the bow. They saw the wherries rise and dive with the sudden waves and the second boy's oar flail out as he fell back into the water.

They saw the first boy fall too, with his oar digging useless into the air and his skull cracking on the edge of the wherry.

He is dead. He was dead before he rolled over the edge and into the lake; before the second boy spluttered up, still laughing.

The director of summer camps stands on the stage, both hands gripping a lectern. He says there will be no more nighttime practice on the water. That tomorrow, before the track meet, we will hold a vigil for the dead boy. That we should learn: mistakes can kill us, even here where the world is safe and ours.

At the end he asks for questions, and a Deck Three girl raises her hand and says, "Will they cancel the Victory Race, again?"

She leaves the pause there, before *again*. Three of her girls look over their shoulders at us. Rose mutters something too soft to hear.

The director shakes his head. "We won't cancel the Victory Race or the Valor Race. We won't cancel wherries. We trust that you'll conduct yourselves with safety, sportsmanship, and style. You'll learn from this. We'll honor that boy, and we know this was a tragedy. But—"

He pauses.

He looks, I'm sure of it, at Deck Five.

He says again what he said before: *Mistakes can kill us.*

We file out with silence holding its hands around our throats.

THE TWO

THAT NIGHT, THE NIGHT with the dead boy, is the first night our door whispers open an hour past taps.

Nisreen stirs, still not asleep, and in the moonlight a tear streaks down her cheek. Flor is a shadow gliding close.

"The counselor—" says Nisreen, softer than breathing.

"She's asleep."

"The lieutenant—"

"Military checks are Deck Two and Deck Four tonight. I heard the counselors talking." Flor pulls the sheet back. Nisreen's blanket is folded down neat: it is hot even now, at midnight, and the breeze is dead and buried. Flor traces her thumb along Nisreen's skin, gentle enough to turn her to silk, and wipes the tear away. She says, "You're crying."

Nisreen eases back toward the wall and lets Flor crawl between the sheets. But still she says, "Mar."

I keep my eyes almost-shut. Flor does not turn to look at me. She weaves her fingers into Nisreen's hair; she molds their shapes together; she murmurs into the dark: *Mar loves us. Mar is one of us.*

It is the way it should be.

THE LEAVE

WE MAKE OUR PLAN in whispers and silence.

We have permit on Saturday: five hours, all ours. We stand at parade rest in the hall, thirty minutes before twelve hundred, not giving it away. In the nervous silence the counselor checks rooms for inspection. We stare hard at the walls opposite our doors, and from down the hall her voice says only, *Gig for dust on the bookcase*, or *gig for pillowcase not folded under.* No one argues. We know better.

Our rooms are last. When the counselor reaches the end of the hall, Rose unlocks the door and pivots back to parade rest. Flor's face is cool and placid.

"Zero gigs," says the counselor, and Rose locks the door again.

After inspection we wait downstairs as parents come in

to sign girls out. We can't leave the grounds alone, but we can leave with staff, and Rose has talked her ensign cousin into lying. He walks us to the end of the lakeshore path. "Rose," he says, "if you get in trouble, it's on you."

She nods.

"You'll be rank-stripped."

She nods.

"You'll—"

"We *know*," says Rose.

He steps back and waits and thinks. He says, "I hope this isn't about—"

"We're going into town," says Rose. "We want to be on our own. You know what it's like first-class summer."

He gives in and walks off.

We are alone, just us.

We step off the lakeshore path and plunge into the wild. The leaves are thick with summer and they swallow up the light but trap the heat, and ahead of me sweat blooms through Nisreen's blouse. The trail clings close to the lake for a narrow quarter-mile, staggering up a bluff with the edge dropping straight to the water.

We burst out of the trees. There is the public beach with a boy perched on the lifeguard stand and children shrieking in the shallows; there is the park with swings swishing. Music plays on radios and cars pass on the road. There are boys running barefoot; there are tangled limbs on towels and girls on the beach, arms around each other, posing for a picture and laughing until they fall.

Across the road, the root beer stand overflows with Marshall. This is where we told Rose's cousin we would be, drinking milkshakes and listening to Rose tell us about a boy. He is the third she has found this summer: the drum major from Naval Band, who is crooked-faced but marches with so much swagger that he always has a whole trail of girls staring after him.

Rose stumbles over nothing and falls against Flor. And Flor stumbles into Nisreen, and Nisreen catches her arm. "You and your boys," says Flor, and Rose blushes a brighter pink than her sunburn, and we laugh, and she doesn't look back at the boy again.

The sidewalk hugs tight against the root beer stand where the road curves uphill. We pass the low wall that hems it in, and one of the Jordanians shouts to Nisreen. She answers fast and laughing.

"What did she say?" Rose asks.

"Where we're going," says Nisreen, her fingers still knotted into Flor's.

"What did you tell her?"

"Home," says Nisreen. "To practice semaphores."

Flor unlaces her hand and shoots her arms out, crisp: *L-I-A-R.*

We climb the hill back up to the road that cuts between the tamed green and the woods: past the gates and the chapel; past the dark grove of the infirmary; past the paddock; around the corner onto East Shore Drive. Lower Camp is buried in trees. Girls hang close to the porches, their sashes proud with badges. Our Dragonfly cabin hides the farthest back of all, but our Butterfly cabin stands halfway up a grassy stretch of hill.

"Deck Five!" shouts a girl on the steps, almost too young to be a Butterfly, and half a dozen other girls prick up and look and see us on the road.

"Cabin Five!" Flor shouts back.

The smallest girl salutes. Her right hand is a knife against her eyebrow. Her sash loops almost to the hem of her skirt.

We salute back and she grins like we are everything.

"Badges sewn close together," says Rose.

We did it, too: stitched our first badges as close as we could, and swore we'd earn so many by the end of Lower Camp that we'd fill two whole sashes without any uniform-blue peeking through.

"I miss those days," says Nisreen, quiet. "Burning up in that cabin, and the mosquitos that bit us all night, and when Mar fainted at Parade."

We laugh and draw in closer, and our strides match without us trying. Nisreen is right: that last Saturday, our first Butterfly summer, I stood so tall in the firing August sun that my knees locked and my vision hazed. And a buzzing, faint and far-off. And I am on the ground, the dead-dry grass poking into my skin, and I am staring at a sky as blue as heaven, and the buzzing comes back, and it is an Aviation boy doing the flyby. He dips his wings and the crowd shouts, and I am smiling, and I taste sweat on my lips, and I think, *I never want to leave this place.*

"Fainting is a gig!" yells Flor, the way she did when the nurse let me out of the infirmary and I walked back to the cabin and found them reading Rose's book of trees, working for their forestry badges. It was: falling out of line, even from fainting, cost us a point in Parade.

We won anyway.

I miss those days, too, when everything was simple and beautiful, and Flor yelled but then they all three wrapped me in their arms and we sat down with the book of trees and read and read while the sky went dark and mosquitos chewed our ankles raw through our socks.

We are still there, I think: sitting on that porch, reading that book, scratching at bug-bites. Singing camp songs to the firefly sky: *In storm and in sunshine, whatever assail, Push onward and conquer and never say fail!*

And I think all at once that if I looked back at those girls who called to us, they would be us four instead.

I look back.

The smallest girl, the one who saluted, still stares after us. Her arms wrap around herself and the smile is gone from her face.

"Come on, hurry up," Rose calls from up ahead.

I turn and run, and Nisreen is running, too, up from a crouch to tie her shoe. Rose and Flor stand waiting where the trees rise up and swallow the road. The space behind them is dark and wanting.

"Hurry *up*!" Rose calls again.

We walk into the dark together. The trees turn the world to silence: no lap of waves on the shore; no faraway shouts from the Butterflies. We walk without speaking. The air is still and simmering with things unsaid.

Last summer, we took this road every Saturday in my father's station wagon, windows down, dragging our hands to cut through the thick air. Our last Saturday, four days before the Victory Race, I leaned my head out the window and tipped it back and stared up as the leaves blurred into rushing green. Rushing green, and light breaking through once and again, and down deep in my stomach there is a dread that claws and grows. Inside the car Nisreen is calling, *Mar, that's dangerous,* and I say *I don't care,* and right when I say it there is a whipping sting across my face, and when I look back a fat bloom of Queen Anne's lace dances from the kiss of my skin against its pinpricked white.

Today we are walking instead, and the blur of the leaves

has gone still. We see every leaf and every branch; every bloom of wild color. The air is thick and thicker.

And then all at once we are there.

We stand poised on the road: sweat-hued blouses and flyaway hair. Rose's gold nametag catches the light cutting down between the trees.

"That boy—" says Nisreen, sudden and hushed.

My breath clutches. High up in the canopy, a breeze moves restless through the leaves. The air hums and threatens.

"The boy who died," she says.

"He was a stupid boy who did a stupid trick," says Rose. "They taught us the first day of Butterflies not to horse around in the water. It's not safe."

"But he *died*," says Nisreen.

"People die," Flor says, and there is a bitter taste to it: a taste like piled roses and black.

"I know," Nisreen answers. There is a taste to how she says it, too, and I wonder who she has lost. In the summer we share whispers and toothpaste and underwear; we know everything about each other. But in the winter we split apart again, and the months pass by full of things we never bring to Lake Nanweshmot.

We are not the same out in the world as we are here on the lake.

We are better here.

"People die," says Nisreen. The breeze flickers again up above but cannot reach us on the ground. "But—there was something so strange about it—"

"What do you mean?" Rose gives her a careful look; a measuring look.

Nisreen sighs and it stirs the weeds behind us. "It was all in a second," she says. "So many things at once, or it wouldn't have happened—"

"You don't mean it was anyone's fault," Rose says, sharper.

Flor steps closer to Nisreen. "Of course she doesn't."

"Because it wasn't," says Rose. "It was an accident. They were showing off, and he fell, and it was awful, but just because it was an accident doesn't undo the consequences."

"They think it was us," says Nisreen, soft. "They think—because of last summer, and Mar—"

"No," says Rose. "We don't need their superstitions. We don't need anyone at all except Deck Five."

We stand in almost silence. We are all, all alone in a patch of sunlight on the edge of East Shore Drive.

Nisreen speaks first. "Let's go," she says, and she takes Flor's hand and crosses the road.

The sound comes back: the birds, and the buzz of the cicadas, and the rustling of the leaves. The lane is narrower than I remember, with branches bending low and ivy crowding in. And my heartbeat skips faster, and I think they might be here after all: my parents, who don't speak with me anymore, not since last summer when they took me away.

Last summer I hated them, and him, and me. But this summer, this summer, I think we will be new again.

The lane is short. In two dozen steps we are rounding the bend with the scent of leaves and lake and—

There. It is there.

The house where I stepped off the pier and plunged into the watercolor. Where we sang happy birthday to Nisreen, the candle-flames glowing brighter every summer. Where time stands still with the sun straight overhead. Where we spin on shining planks in our saddle-shoes, where we shriek mad and wonderful at each other, where we doze on the porch with our legs honeyed gold and our hair glossed in sunlight.

"God," says Flor, and she is almost praying it. "I miss—"

And suddenly nothing matters: not the lies or the boy who died or the boy from last summer. I am running, we are running, like the thought came over all of us at once, and we glaze past the house and down the slope of grass and onto the shore. We are tugging at our shoes, we are pulling at the buttons on our blouses, we are shedding our last-summer shells and running for the water, we are shouting like wild girls. We churn the lake into diamonds that fly up into the bright, and we swim out far, and we dig our toes into the mud, and we float on our backs and let the sky come down and take us in.

We are water and sky and girls. There is nothing else but us.

THE STORM

ROSE SAYS, AFTER NEVER-LONG-ENOUGH, "We should go back."

Flor stands silhouetted, squinting toward the north shore. The water comes up to her ribs and her dark hair clings to her shoulders. One white bra-strap hangs careless over her arm. She shrugs it back up and says, "The flags."

Rose stands up next to her, and Nisreen and I float close. From out here we can just see the Naval Building peeking past the shore and the code-flags snapping on the line. The sky is bright but gray. To the west a darkness stands waiting.

"Does it mean anything?" Flor asks.

I read the flags: *Golf, November, Three.*

"Yes," says Rose. "It means two hours until lineup."

It doesn't, but we head for the shore anyway.

Our clothes are a pile on the beach and we sift through them and shake the damp away. Nisreen stands with her arms flung out, embracing the whole world, and the water traces rivulets down her legs and pools at her feet. Flor watches; drinks her in; lets her shoes and socks fall back onto the ground; wraps herself close around Nisreen.

"You'll get caught, you know," says Rose.

"No we won't," says Flor. "We're nowhere. No one knows we're here."

Rose wrings the water from her curls. "You'll get caught some night you think they're not doing checks, or some morning sneaking back into our room."

"Mar went sneaking out every night last summer and never got caught." Flor says it like I never hid it from them; as though I carved his name into our tree.

"Don't," says Rose. "You know the way it ended."

Last summer a boy said, *Will you keep us a secret?* Last summer I said *yes* and *yes* and *yes*.

"Everything ends," Flor says, unheeding, and she seals her lips and Nisreen's. They kiss so full and brilliant Rose has to look away.

We wander off, Rose and me, weaving onto the mossy bumps of the boat ramp. Above our heads the sign stands familiar: SHADY BLUFF. Great hanging spiderwebs drape down from it, and higher up, the winter shutters are rolled tight.

"Where are they?" Rose asks, barely murmuring it.

I want to run back into the lake and dive down to where only sifting sunshine can find me. When we were in the water nothing had changed. Here on the shore the windows are tucked away even with July shouting. The words bleed in from that night in the storm: my mother's voice, *It's time to go,* and it is a coffin cracking shut.

A gust kicks across the lake and peels water-drops off our skin. Rose turns. "Damn," she says, and she sounds like her father. "Should've known better. *Damn.*"

"What?" Flor asks. Her shorts hang loose and unzipped on her hips. Nisreen crouches on the rocks, gathering tiny shells and dropping them into the heel of one shoe.

Rose points out over the lake. Far off above the west shore, the sky has gone black. Lightning flicks at the treetops and whitecaps whip up and roil.

"Get dressed," says Rose, and she shakes her hair out like a dog. "We'll have to run if we want to make it back before the storm."

Nisreen looks over the water. "We won't make it," she says.

"Don't," says Rose, raw, and I feel the dread again. "This is different."

We have no time but we stand frozen anyway, watching the storm rise up. The sky was clear when we climbed the hill out of town. But that is the way it is here: a sky bright blue one hour, and the next the wind lashes hard enough to break limbs from trees. Rain streams down over the west shore already, and I know that in the grand old Victorian far across from Shady Bluff, there is the slam of windows shutting it out.

"Let's go in," says Flor.

"We can't," says Rose. "Not by ourselves."

"God," says Flor. "It's Mar's house, too."

I tell them, the way I always do, that it is ours. All of us. It's still true, I think, even with it shut against us.

"Come on," says Flor. "We wanted to anyway."

Across the lake the rain advances. The boats have scattered. Four piers away, the father and children from the yellow house with the flat lawn are scrambling out of their scow and letting down the sail. It ruffles deafening in the wind and they shout over it, grabbing for ties, tossing life vests onto the pier. A bolt of lightning shoots down over the trees and spreads ten fingers out.

"Come *on*," says Flor, and she gathers us up with the pull of her words. The wind tears in. We run for the grass and it is long and shot through with weeds my mother would never let grow, and the sting at my ankles makes it real in a way it was not before.

"Come on!" This time Rose says it, shouting, because Nisreen and I are dawdling again. Staring out at the storm. It crawls closer, and churns up the lake, and the whipping sail four houses down has tamed, but instead there is the snapping of the flags at the end of every pier: the stars and stripes next door, and the Marshall M beyond it. And far away and out of sight the code-flags on the Naval Building, *Golf November Three*, and the meaning comes back to me, useless: *Can you take off persons?* When we first read it, some Dragonfly summer, Rose said, *Take off persons. What does it even mean?* And Flor laughed where she perched on our cabin steps and said, *Throw a man into the sea.*

"I found it!" she yells now over the wind, and the storm is bearing down. We run after her with our blouses bundled in our arms. Flor has dug under the flowerpot beside the kitchen door. She has the key in her hand, tarnished but victorious, and she trips up the steps and flings the screen door back. The wind catches it and slams it against the rail.

"No," says Nisreen, and Rose shouts *what?*, and we are wet skin and tangled hair, bunched up on the step, and Flor has the key in the lock. Out on the lake the rain consumes the piers.

"No," says Nisreen. "We shouldn't be here. It isn't right. It—"

Lightning explodes like fireworks and war, and thunder knocks our jaws shut, and rain covers us so thick we choke on it.

Flor turns the knob and pushes through the door. We fall in after her, Rose and me, slipping barefoot on the wood.

"Get inside!" Flor shouts in the strange quiet. Nisreen still stands on the stoop, showered in storm.

"Nisreen! God, you crazy girl, you—" And Flor reaches back out and pulls Nisreen in, and Rose fights the screen and slams both doors.

Flor is scattering laughter and shaking Nisreen and kissing her hair and her skin and her lips. And Rose *tsks* and says we'll all die of pneumonia, and we go to the linen closet and dig out towels and blankets and pile them where we washed up in the kitchen nook.

We hang our uniforms over chair-backs to hope the wrinkles away. Rose smacks at them and Nisreen's little shells click out: spirals and whorls and clams as small as fingernails. We tuck towels around our ribs and wrap up in blankets. They are bright and hideous, knit by my grandmother with her knobbing knuckles and her peppermint-scent from the candies in her pockets. Bright and hideous, and worn, and they smell like dust but like last summer too, and when I was a little lake-girl tucked safe in their sunset color with the windows open and night wafting in.

"It's full of ghosts," says Nisreen.

"Why would you *say* that?" Rose flicks a towel at her and the snap echoes in the quiet. Outside the storm beats down, and the windows blur like stained glass, and there is too much dark leaking in from the porch.

"Look," says Nisreen. She is at the kitchen door, her

thin shoulders poking out above orange and gold and white yarn.

We come up behind her.

Ahead of us the house is spotless-clean, not even the dust there should be, and with a shine to the wide plank floor. White sheets drape over the dining-room table and the couch and the recliner where my father sits smoking, reading, nodding. The little stool beside it is a small ghost, like Nisreen said, and it is bare. It is never bare: it is stacked tall, always, with books and journals and *The New Yorker*, and a ceramic ashtray I made in Butterflies. When I gave it to him my mother laughed so hard she cried and said, *That's art, right there*, but my father kissed me on the forehead and said, *I love it, Margaret, it's useful*, and set the lumpy thing next to his books, and Shady Bluff took it in.

It is missing now. The books and the magazines; the lingering cigar-smoke; the ugly tray I made. It is as though Shady Bluff has shed part of itself away.

"It's too empty, that's all," says Rose, louder than she should.

I tell them it is always like this before summer starts, when it is barely May and still wanting to snow. We pull back the sheets and fold them together, like color-guard girls tucking the flag into a triangle of white and red. We knock the shutters away and ask the summer in. We turn the radio on and let music stream through the house: jazz and old dance-songs and songs about love; songs about summertime.

"It's already summer," says Nisreen, hanging back. "They should be here."

"They should," Rose says. "And at Parade every week, sitting with my parents—and coming for us in the car, instead of us creeping around like we don't belong when we *do*—"

Flor turns. She is by the fireplace and the bookshelves; by the walls hung with photographs. Behind her, in the glass, her reflection stands hands on hips. "Did we think it would be the same?"

Thunder lands again when she says it, still close enough to rattle us.

"No," says Nisreen. "But—" She sighs and it shudders, like she has been crying.

I come back to her until she draws in a deep breath and comes out into the house.

We wander the empty rooms with the rain pouring down. Even in the hollow of it, it is still Shady Bluff. The blankets; the photographs: my mother and father with their heads leaning in together over little-girl-me, the summer I stepped backward off the pier. My grandmother, before she died, in the shade on the lawn with needles in her hands, spinning the blanket Rose wears now. My Marshall portraits and my father's, too. And us, us girls, in the Butterfly days with our sashes and real smiles.

"The clock stopped," says Rose, by the mantel. We look. The hands are stuck at noon exactly, pointing straight to the sky. Rose nudges them around to ten minutes past three.

"It's dead," says Flor, at the door to the sunporch.

"I know," says Rose. "But it can still be right."

"Look out here." Flor has rattled on already, pulling open the door and letting out the dusk. The smell of waiting rot seeps out. "It's so dark."

She disappears inside and there is a crash and a curse and behind me, Nisreen laughs. "I can hear you!" Flor shouts. "You'd fall too. And I stubbed my stupid toe."

And we all laugh, instead of just Nisreen, because Flor is summer-Flor now. Freer even than she is back at Marshall, where everyone can see her and tell someone who will tell her father.

"Come on," she says. The rain is fainter, and the windows gaze brighter, and we have made it through the storm, I think.

We come into the dark. There is the dimmest buzz of the shutters shaking against the glass. The pressing wood planks make my lungs hitch like we are shut in with nothing to breathe.

"We should open it up," Flor is saying, tracing her fingers down the glass. "It shouldn't be shut up all summer."

I wander off to the south side of the porch. My favorite corner, jutting out enough to see the steeple high up above the green. Enough to see the *H.H. Bedford* moored past the Naval Pier. She is a tall square-rigger caught in Lake Nanweshmot, sailing in circles. We made apprentice-crew last summer and learned the ropes. Every day we climbed the masts and swung high and blind in the sun, letting out the sheets and swatting at the fat gray spiders that skittered up our arms.

"Put the shutters up," Flor says, and it echoes in the dark like a dream. "It feels like a grave."

I find my place in the corner. The glass hums.

It feels like—secrets, says Flor.

And everything splits like the tree lightning struck our third-class summer. One night it was whole. The next morning it was sliced in half, flayed open to tender flesh not meant to be seen.

Flor says—and she is far away—she says, *Let the light back in*—and it is caught in amber with the words she said out on the beach: *Mar went sneaking out every night last summer and never got caught.* She has always known but still she is wrong. They caught me and they came for me and I should never have come back to this forsaken house where time hangs dead and broken—

I run out from the corner and the porch. The door is too heavy and the deadbolt sticks, and I can't get out, and that is what I want, isn't it? I said to them, *I don't want to leave,* I said *Don't take me away,* and the car is speeding through the dark, and the storm is back.

I am trapped—
I don't want to leave—
And the storm—

THE FORGOTTEN

IT IS SECOND-CLASS SUMMER again
and we are full of promise
and every Saturday we come to Shady Bluff
and every week Rose has found a new boy
and every week Flor and Nisreen have found each other
and every week I bind my secret close to me, because I love him and he knows more than I do, with his father on the Marshall board; with his great sprawling mansion on the shore of Lake Michigan where the rich boys live; with his grand old Victorian on Lake Nanweshmot; with his eyes the tempting dark of the lake late at night; with his ribbon-rack all full of honors stacked row after row; with the way he said, when winter bloomed to spring, *I love you, Mar.*

It is second-class summer again and we have a secret.

Not the *we* I have always been in Neverland. We, him and me, and no one knows but us. We are us in the dark, sneaking out on nights the counselors leave the doors propped open, jamming bubble-gum into the locks so we can slip back in after. We are us on the shore, hidden in the secret spot where every pair of Marshall lovers hides to watch the sunset, but the sunset belongs to all of them and the starlight is ours alone. We are us trading glances from the foremast of the *H.H. Bedford* to the main, bound up into the sky by the secret of it. We are us from that lakeshore walk at the sweet bitter end of our third-class summer. We are us in the long cold night between August and June, and no one ever talks from the last day of one summer to the first day of the next, because it is tradition.

It is second-class summer again and we broke tradition and spun our two summers together. Third and second, and his and mine. Spun them with threads made from the heavy ropes on the *H.H. Bedford*, and from the spider silk that crosses the lakeshore path and catches the dew, and from the flax-strands the leaves pull from my scalp when we make our hideaway on that little point at midnight.

It is second-class summer again and my heart could burst with pride at who we have become, and my soul is strung with a love like no one in the world has ever known, I'm sure of it. With our long long talks that melted the ice of February and made it spring, with our whole selves bared open like that lightning-struck tree, with his words he has told no one but me: *I will never be the man my father wants me to be.* It is something any Marshall boy could say, but only one will say it out loud and only one will be—I know it—will be what his father wants him to be and even more. He is beautiful and bright and aching to be great; he is perfect but still uncertain underneath it, no matter how wide his smile and how stunning-sure he is, spinning rifles in the Honor Guard or crouching at the helm, cutting sails into the wind to steal the Valor Race for Naval One.

It is second-class summer again and he is a boy and a comet in the sky, passing by not once in a lifetime but once in a hundred of them. It is second-class summer again and I am a poet and a dreamer and a girl who sees the good in everyone, a girl who wants to live in color so bright it should never last but it will for us: we know it.

It is second-class summer again and it is ours, and time stands still for us, and we are stronger than tradition and truer than secrets

and I love him
and he loves me
and I would die for him if I could, I think
and he would kill for me
and I say *I love you*
and he says it too
and we won't tell

we won't tell
we won't

THE CONSEQUENCES

WE ARE NOT IN trouble.

We are not late.

We cut back across the grounds, through the Lower Camp woods and out by the pier; along the lakeshore path to Neverland. We are back in time for lineup, and we march to the mess for supper, and when girls whisper we look through them like they are not there. We drill for an hour in the blaze of evening light. We march onto the parade field with our shoulders back and four flags streaming over our heads: Military and Athletic and Naval and the best honor of all, Deck Five.

We don't lose our lines when we pivot to cross in front of the lakehouse parents in the stands. We don't faint in all the hot waiting before it, with a plane buzzing low for the flyby. We scream in the earsplitting echoes of the tunnel: *Our veins bleed orange, our hearts are gold.*

We gather after, under the trees on the Admiral's Walk, and line up again to march home. And the lieutenants come over, with the director, and they are here to tell us we have won Parade again, and we have earned it.

We stand at attention. We are proud because we should be.

The director says, “I need to see a few of your girls.”

We know who we are before he calls our names.

We walk after him as our deck fades onto the lakeshore path. Our steps still match their cadence. The evening is sinking in and the brick buildings shimmer out the heat of day.

His office is exactly above the tunnel, with windows looking out over the parade field on one side and the east quad on the other. He sits at an oak desk and flags frame him: the stars and stripes and the Marshall M. We are all in a row on a shining-stiff chesterfield. Our backs are straight.

We are not in trouble.

He lets us have a long silence made for confession. We leave it unopened.

He says at last, “You will not leave the grounds unchaperoned again.”

We take his words without lowering our chins.

He says, “Do you understand?”

We say, *Sir, yes, sir.*

He says, “In particular, you will not go to a lakehouse uninvited.”

Rose says, because she is a Winston, “But Margaret—”

Flor's heel comes down hard on the toe of Rose's saddle-shoe. I swallow slow and deliberate. The room is much too hot.

"What about Margaret?" he asks.

We don't answer.

"Is there anything you'd like to tell me about the Moore house?"

We say, *Sir, no, sir.*

"Have you spoken with Margaret's parents?"

We say, *Sir, no, sir.*

He waits. He looks past us, out over the green, toward the pier and the shore and the lake. "I'd hoped we could leave the past in the past. Was I wrong?"

We say, *Sir, no—*

"Sir," says Rose. Flor stomps at her foot again; drives it into the rug. "With respect, we aren't the ones keeping secrets."

Even being a Winston isn't enough to let her say it.

"Rose," he says, "I'd hate to see you rank-stripped your first-class summer."

"Sir," she says, and Flor presses down harder, and Rose slides her toe out from under Flor's heel. "With respect—"

"Is it?"

"With *respect*, sir, you can go ahead and take my rank. You already sent us home once because we wouldn't sit down and be quiet and stop asking questions—"

"Miss Winston," he says. Outside the window the leaves move, silent. He wants something from us and it feels unsafe, I think. Like there is something to dig up from last summer and place on his desk, writhing in the sudden light, and pulling us down again when we have fought and fought to be here. "Are your girls also willing to sacrifice their ranks?"

Her fingers press into the leather of the sofa. He is using us against her and he is prying at us, to pry us apart, because apart we are only one and one and one and one, and together we are too much for him to understand at all.

Flor says, "Sir, yes, sir."

He blinks. "Pardon?"

She stands up. She salutes. "Sir, we're willing to sacrifice our ranks, sir."

He sits back in his chair. "All of you."

We say, *Sir, yes, sir.*

And that is it: that is what it takes. He won't strip our ranks after all, because we have given them away, and because we are united. Without looking each other in the eye; without a spat between Rose and Flor. Rose has the easy luxury of a father who will sigh and say, *Really, Mary Rose?*, but then they will take the scow out and win the regatta, and later on the lawn he will laugh about it with her uncles, and they will say, *Back in Marshall days*, and tell stories about liquor flasks and streaking on the drill-field.

Rose has a father who will say, *Well, damn. She's a*

Winston through and through. Flor has a father who will say nothing, and it will be worse than anything he could say, because honor for her is more than the Marshall code. It is family and party and all she will ever want.

But Flor has her right hand sharp against her eyebrow and she has put everything on the line for us.

The director says, "Girls, I'm disappointed."

Flor orders-arms and sits, victorious.

He says, "Not that you've spoken back, and not even that you broke the rules. I'm disappointed that you won't put Marshall before yourselves. This place is something greater than any one of us alone. It's bigger than you, Miss Al-Shayab—or Miss Gómez, or Miss Winston—"

He leans on the silence. He is prying again, and he has found the raw place.

"Or Miss Moore," he says.

It means too much.

"Tonight," he says, "think about what it means to be part of this tradition."

We leave one after the next, saluting the way we must and looking higher than his eyes. Out through the swirling leaves, the color-guard girls lower the flag in the long light.

We are not in trouble.

We are in something worse.

I AM MARGARET MOORE

THE NIGHT-TIME

THAT NIGHT THE MOON rises so full it seems ready to burst. Its light spills out over the ink-black sky and paints the sycamores across the lawn. The lake is smooth and flat with no wind to sail. And the moon shines back again from the water, so blinding bright I almost can't look at it.

It is quieter than I knew the world could be. No waves lap against the shore and no crickets chirp. And it is beautiful: so beautiful that the breath catches between my ribs. It struggles and grows long-nailed fingers that scratch against bone until finally all the air rushes out of me and my eyes smart hard with water and stars.

I have to turn my back. There is something fearsome out in the bright silence of the night. There is a knowing and a wanting; there is something stirring under the stillness. There is change cracking and groaning underneath the ever-sameness of the summer.

I can't look at it. I can't think of it. It is too beautiful and too eternal and too fleeting.

It is too much, and I am not enough.

HANNAH CAPIN

THE RETURN

AFTER, IT IS AS though nothing has happened.

The days are a rank that never breaks. The whole camp knows we were called in, and they talk, and we do not tell even Deck Five. They are locked out of our secrets, but still they stand up for us when a Naval Three boy noses into our line at the mess and says, *If your first classmen keep breaking rules, you'll never win the Victory Race.* It hurts me, down in the marrow of my bones, to know we are hurting them—hurting *us*, our Deck Five girls.

Everything is the way it should be. We line up. We march. We drill. We sail. In class we learn archery and horsemanship; celestial navigation; how to reef the *H.H. Bedford* for a gale. After class we stay to ourselves, swinging semaphores and hoisting code-flags and flipping fast through *The International Code of Signals.* We row wherries where that boy died. We don't pray for him, because he is not our fault.

The cicadas buzz louder and louder. The heat dries up the sweat on our skin and turns the grass stiff and thirsting.

And Rose finds a new boy, and Flor and Nisreen find each other, and I keep my eyes ahead and my chin high and I do not look for him.

THE FOURTH

ALL AT ONCE IT is the Fourth of July, and we are sitting down on the sagging wooden bleachers by the horsemanship building, waiting for dark. Half the town lounges on blankets, and children shriek and run in circles. The band plays. The bell tolls. The cannon on the lakeshore puffs gray smoke. The Honor Guards drill: first the girls, flawless, and not one dropped rifle. And then the boys, and I look out at the boats anchored past the Island, glowing red and green and white.

Rose and Flor climb back into their seats halfway through the boys' show and Rose says, breathless, "They're here. Mar's parents."

Nisreen looks over her shoulder.

"Don't!" Rose says between her teeth.

"Why not?" Flor looks too.

Then we all look, and Rose says, "Under the tree. By that man with the binoculars—"

"Oh!" says Nisreen, and then they snap back to the field. There is a tide of applause for the Honor Guard boys and I won't look for him. Instead I am looking, still, at my parents.

They are here.

And I think there is hope after all, and they are here for the summer at last.

The man beside them sets his binoculars down and says something to my father and my father nods and smiles—almost smiles; a smile for him.

The man beside him lives in a great sprawling mansion on Lake Michigan and a grand old Victorian on Lake Nanweshmot. He is a good man: the oldest son of the third great Marshall family, with the Winstons and the Bedfords. A man who could pay for anything, and he has.

He claps my father on the shoulder. His wife is smiling, and my mother is smiling, and they are watching the boys march off the field. And they cheer: my father and my mother, and his father and his mother.

The director is on the field again, shouting loud into his microphone: "Let's have another round of applause for our boys in the Honor Guard—"

I am stumbling up and tripping over Flor and Rose. Behind us the Naval Four boys leap to their feet with their knees knocking into our backs, shouting a cheer like they always do, and I fall against a second classman. A counselor calls, "In your seats, in your seats," and Naval Four shouts louder—

Naval Four, Naval Four, find us on the Lake Nan shore
Where you bet we'll meet a—
Horrible, huge mistake, wreck our boats out on the lake—

"In your seats," the director says over his microphone, but he was Naval Four thirty summers ago and he is almost laughing. I stand up, find my footing—

Then the sky is aflame and the world is on its feet. Everything is fireworks and bright. It is Independence Day and it is our first-class summer and they are back and they are with him.

I am on my feet. I am pushing past Rose and Flor. The sky fades to black and then shoots bright again, orange and glowing, and the crowd cheers.

I am on the stairs and grabbing at the rail. I am calling for Rose, for Flor, for Nisreen. But the fireworks are gunfire and the band is playing again, the Navy fight song, fast and loud and chaos.

No one can hear me. It is swallowing me up, the noise and the lights, and it is my fault, and I feel for the next step in the blinding dark, and my shoe is catching, and I fall.

It is daylight all at once

and the sky is blue and streaked with a single plane buzzing overhead

and I am a Butterfly

and I am lying on my back with the grass poking at my thighs

and I taste sweat on my lips

and I have never loved and never lost, never lied, never

and I never want to leave this place.

HANNAH CAPIN

THE FAIRYTALE

I LOVED A BOY once, before all this. I loved him so strong and so true I can feel it still, braiding me together and tearing me apart. So that all the world was beautiful and bright, and all the world was endless possibility, and all the world was only us and we were meant to be.

His name was—

Nothing.

His name was *him* and my name was *her* and together, together we were *us*. His smile was wide and bright. His hands were strong. He tasted like sunlight and he looked at me like I was everything. We kissed in the curve of the oldest tree in the park on evenings when the world was still dark, and the warmth between us melted winter to spring. His lips against my cheek, against my hair, against my neck. His breath against my ear:

I love you, Margaret.

The days burned brighter and the flowers bloomed, and the sky turned a watery light-blue that lingered later every night. And he said:

I'll always love you.

I kissed him like I was drowning and he was the shore. We drank whiskey he stole from his father's desk drawer and my laugh was high and bubbling. I wanted his hands on me. I wanted my hands on him. It was April the first day we caught each other up in the last row of the old theater and tangled together in one seat, breathless and alive. The day we fumbled and laughed and crushed our hands over each other's mouths while the projector's light blazed above us. And he said:

God, Mar, how did I ever get lucky enough to be born in the same world as you?

And we kissed like the world would end. And my skirt slid up high and I found the buckle on his belt and we'd never talked about it, never gotten close, but it was the only thing we wanted. Then he was inside me and hurt sparked like stars but it didn't matter because he was there with his arms wrapped tight around me and his lips on mine. We were real. We were whole. We were *us*. And he said:

I love you, Mar, I love you.

And I said:

I'm yours.

And we made us and we ruined us.

HANNAH CAPIN

THE CAGE

I WAKE IN THE dark.

There is a blur I half-remember: lights and fussing, and a Lower Camp girl hopping on one leg with blood trailing down the other, and the nurse saying, *It's always the Fourth, isn't it?*

I sit up. I am on a thin mattress with blue sheets and the walls are a faded sick green. There is no door to my room.

See you in the morning, says a voice downstairs. *Get some rest.*

I sit back against the wall. The paint is cool and almost damp, and above me the window is open to the night and the crickets chirp so loud they could wake the boy who died.

Across the hall, through the dark, someone cries out in sleep.

I have been here only twice before—here, the upstairs of the infirmary, where the overnight patients sleep. Both times we were visiting Nisreen when she was locked away: once with a fever that made her see ghosts, and once when a rash ran so fast up her leg they thought her blood was poisoned. She told us her room was haunted, and Flor laughed until an older girl said Nisreen was right, and long ago a boy died here at the end of the hall.

We don't believe in ghosts, but still we stay away. It is far from everything and lonely, and smelling like bleach. There is too much time to think.

I stand and find my balance. The crickets sing and moonlight shifts through the leaves. On my tiptoes I can see out the window, through the branches and down the hill to where my parents sat with that boy's father. The space there beneath the tree brings the hurt back, a low ache that clutches in my stomach.

I step back from the window. My blouse is dirty. My saddle-shoes are scuffed on one toe from something I don't remember: something long ago, that night in the storm. Across the room there is a porcelain sink with a mirror nailed over it, green-tinged and with rust spots spoiling from the corners.

The girl across the hall cries out *Don't,* plaintive and clear.

I turn. She is sitting up in her bed, looking out through the hall and into my room. She is a Butterfly with the sheets pulled up to her chin. Her eyes are circled in shadow.

She says, *Get out.*

I look into the hall. Far down at the other end, one

lightbulb flickers over the linoleum. I ask what's wrong, and the Butterfly says again, *Get out,* and she is rocking back and forth.

She doesn't see anything; she doesn't mean anything. She is murmuring through a fever-dream, the way Nisreen did all those summers ago. She is burning hot and warning me about nothing.

She is a Butterfly. I am a first classman. If I were brave like Nisreen or strong like Flor or bold like Rose I would go in and tell the Butterfly there is nothing to fear. I would tell her she is safe here, safe now: nine years old and going home to her cabin tomorrow. That she must trust her Butterfly girls, and tell them everything.

I would sit beside her bed until we banished all her ghosts.

But I am not brave or strong or bold. I am a girl who daydreams and falls in love too fast. I am blinking the haze from my eyes and trying, trying to be half of what I am when I am one of us. I am slipping out into the hall and leaving the Butterfly behind.

I look into her room once more before I go.

She is curled in a ball with her pillow clutched against her chest, sleeping sound and deep.

I AM MARGARET MOORE

THE CALL

I STEAL BACK INTO Neverland long past taps. They are there in the hall, waiting for me, gathered tight around the phone we are not allowed to use except on Saturdays.

I sit against the wall and bring my knees to my chest. Nisreen sits down beside me. I cannot get too close to the phone without that night creeping up into my throat and buzzing in my ears.

Rose has the phone in her hand. She looks at me, and she is asking permission, and I do not say no because I do not know how to say why. I want to know, anyway, the same as they do: why my parents have not come back to Shady Bluff; why they sat beneath a tree and did not speak to me. Why they laughed with that man who would turn me to nothing.

I want to know but I cannot ask, because then I would have to tell.

Flor says, and it is low and urgent, "This is crazy. Hang up right now."

And Rose says, "Damn it, Flor, do you have a better idea?"

And Flor says, "It's oh-two-hundred hours, *Rose,* do

you think anyone answers the phone at oh-two-hundred hours?"

Rose drops coins into the slot and in the silence they slice like a guillotine blade.

"Shh!" Flor hisses.

Rose pokes the numbers in. She is calling Shady Bluff.

"Hang up," says Flor again.

"It's ringing," Rose whispers back.

They look at me. I look away.

"What do you want them to say?" Nisreen asks, finally.

The hall is so dead-quiet I can hear the ringing through the receiver, and it rings and rings the way it did last summer when I sat with my hands pressed over my ears and Nisreen said, *Mar, what's wrong?*. The floor shines like water: wavering, shivering.

"What Mar can't," Rose says, and it smarts. "That there was a boy. That he was why they kicked her out."

I want to tell them all the rest. But still my memory blurs and spots, and every time I begin to think of that night in the storm the dread rises up and I know: the more I remember, the more we will be unsafe.

"And why they were here," says Rose, "and why they aren't back at Shady Bluff—"

The phone still rings. If I listen hard I can hear it shrilling in the empty rooms and soaking into the sheets.

"But what are you going to *say*?" Flor asks, pushing

closer. "'Hello, Dr. Moore, hello, Mrs. Moore, this is Rose Winston calling, and we wanted to ask you all about the night Mar—'"

Rose cracks the phone back into the receiver. The sound flips down the hall and we wait, breathless, for doors to fly open.

No one stirs. The echo dies.

"I'm sorry," says Rose, and she falls back against the wall and slides down until she is sitting, and Flor sits, too, so it is the four of us knee to knee. "Calling them doesn't make sense. I *know* that."

Nisreen says, quiet, "They don't know the truth we want, anyway."

We sit in silence. The phone and my lies hang over us.

We go to bed without another word.

THE BALANCE

HERE IS WHAT I know:

Last summer I ran out into the storm to meet the boy I loved.

Last summer my girls ran after me.

Last summer I had to go away, and it was not my choice,

and I could never tell my side of it, and he could tell them anything he wanted, and he did.

Here is what I do not know:

The things he said

and the things that happened after that night when I was gone away

and why they sent our whole deck home

and why nothing at all has happened to him, with all that has happened to me

and what he will do if I give up his name

and what they will do if we tell—

THE TRAP

ROSE HAS FOUND A boy. He is the tenth boy she has found this summer, or the twelfth, or the thirteenth.

She swears this one is different; this one is *real.*

"I'll tell you at dinner," she says, her voice high and hopeful as we slap our palms against the M.

"We'll die of suspense," says Flor, flat, still pinning her nametag into place.

"*Stop,*" Rose says. Laughing down the stairs. "Just because you're already in love—"

"You don't love him," says Flor. "You didn't even notice him until yesterday." She falls into step with Nisreen. Even not leaning their heads on each other's shoulders, even not trailing their hands along each other's skin, they are as inseparable as anything could be.

We are outside now, and lining up, and Rose says, "I'm not being dramatic. It's different this time. And—"

She is radiant. She is breathless and pink-cheeked under her wealth of freckles. "He likes me too."

"Let the earth stand still," says Flor.

Today Rose is the first to our table. She is too excited to eat; too excited to keep from looking over her shoulder. Today the boys marched in first and they are rowdy and laughing.

"*Look* at him," she says without saying who.

"How handsome," says Flor. She kicks Nisreen under the table.

"You don't even know who I mean!"

"That Aviation boy from the first week?" Nisreen asks, hiding her smile behind her hand.

"No," says Flor. "The drum major."

And we fall over each other to name all the boys she loathes now that she has found their imperfections. *No, he doesn't stand up straight!* Rose retorts, or *No, he can't sail at* ALL.

Finally she looks again and says, "There."

Nisreen looks. Flor scoops a spoonful of peas.

"Look!" says Rose, grabbing Flor's elbow.

Across the mess, the boys' bat officers stand up from their place at the center table.

"That red-haired one?" Flor asks, innocent, about the Naval Three boy who shouted, then cried, then stomped away the time we raced boys and girls together in Lower Camp and our canoe beat the best boys by half a length.

"No!" Rose cries out. She pulls us close, as though the whole deck won't know who it is by supper. "Him. See, he's looking—don't look, don't look!"

Her head pokes up again and she wears her UC posture, shoulders squared, but with a grin across her face.

"My *God*, you are *impossible*," says Flor, going back to her peas.

"Which one?" says Nisreen.

"Him!" says Rose, and I am almost looking away again too, because no matter how much she swears and blushes now, he will be forgotten in a day.

The knot of boys unties itself and there he stands. Bat com this week, but he wears it like he is reg com, and somehow also like he is any boy in his company and not an officer at all.

He is beautiful and bright and aching to be great.

Rose says, *Look at him, look, he's looking at me!*

He is. He is smiling like there is no one else in the room but them.

Looking at her like she is the world.

THE RECKONING

I AM OUT OF the mess so early I am sure the sternest woman on the military staff, Lieutenant Caldwell, will stop me. She is always, *Young lady, walk, don't run;* she is always, *Young lady, sit with your deck until they've finished their dinner.* But today she says nothing.

I am humming with a high wild fear. I am walking the edge of the parade field. Dragonflies shout on the shore, *Do you have the paddles? Don't let them take the best boat!*, and the sun burns and burns.

I am walking, running, walking, and it is only my uniform holding me together. If one lace came untied, if one button came loose, I would fall apart into a thousand pieces and blow away onto the lake.

Up in the chapel the carillon bells burst to life. Ringing a whole long song instead of the chiming of the hour: ringing the way they do after Sunday service.

Today they ring only for me.

I take the hill to the chapel. The door is propped wide and fans blow at the heavy air in the vestibule. The bells chime louder.

I climb into heat like hell, up to the room with the keyboard. The organist sits at the bench and the girls and boys who sing in the choir wilt against the walls and fan themselves with black folders, and still I climb.

When I step into the carillon the last note tolls. The sound still fills the room like water, and down below the organist says something and a choir-girl replies, slow and languid in the heat.

It is too hot to stand; too loud to think. I sit down with the bells all around me, dying away, with only the echoes to speak for them.

I said nothing to Rose about the boy. I sat in silence, the way I did last summer in that grand old Victorian. The way I did those last spiraling days when they asked again and again, *Mar, what is it? Tell us what's wrong.* And here I am again with last summer crushing me to nothing, so much I cannot even think it; so much I cannot tell.

I am angry. I am so angry I can hear it in the buzzing in my skull. In the pit of my stomach there is a curdling yell that would split Marshall in two if I let it out. There is a truth that would hurt that boy the same way he hurt me.

I do not scream. I sit, silent, as the echoes fade. As my ears sing from the noise of it.

My hands press against the stone. It is hot with its own heartbeat.

I don't want to think of the time before. It is worse than the things that came after, to remember the times we were happy. But it is too hot and I am tired, sick-tired, from the silence and the fear and what I forget and what I remember.

It is too hot and I am too tired not to remember and not to think of it; of him; of us.

THE WINTER

I LOVED A BOY once, before all this. I loved him so strong and so true that it changed me and turned me real. So that it changed the whole world and everything in it: the old park down the street from my house, and all the secret places Marshall held for us, and the cities I had only seen in books and dreams.

His name was—

Nothing.

No: that is wrong.

His name was everything.

He was, he is, a boy from a family with promises to

keep. He was a boy who walked Marshall like he owned it, even our third-class summer. A boy the director knew and answered when that boy said, *How are you, sir?* in the whirling triumph after Parade.

We kissed, that first night we spoke, on the shore of Lake Nanweshmot.

We strung our summers together, August to June. October, leaves crunching beneath our shoes, walking the quiet streets of my little almost-Chicago town, with the dark coming down and the lights blazing up in dining-room windows. January, kissing and kissing in his new car until the windows turned to fog. April, in the shy green of spring, walking out of the old movie theater where we had our fumbling laughing first time. His arm around me and mine around him.

He said, *Margaret Moore, you are something else.*

We kissed once more, through his rolled-down window, and he drove away into the sunset and back to his cold house on Lake Michigan. I had been there only once, the day the air unfroze in March and we drove and drove all afternoon. No one was home and I gazed up the spiral staircase with snow melting off my shoes while he ran up to get the books he wanted to return to the college where my father taught. *Might as well grab them,* he said, and I felt the thrill of what he left unsaid: *you are invited.*

But it was late already, and too close to evening to wait for his mother and father. *You'll meet them soon,* he said,

Or summer. Permit weekends—you'll come to The Poplars, won't you?

I said yes. I said yes always: when he said, *Will you walk with me?* When he said, hands playing on the buttons of my cardigan, *Will you let me see you?* When he said, that night after I stood waiting in the cavern of his house, *Will you keep us a secret?*

I said yes, because I loved him. I said yes, because he loved me.

So we kept us our secret, and it was keen and everything, and I read *Romeo and Juliet*, I read sonnets, I read Emily Dickinson out loud in the nook of our tree in the park:

Wild nights - Wild nights!
Were I with thee
Wild nights should be
Our luxury!

He laughed when I read poetry; when I pulled the words apart and wondered at them. He said, *Wild nights, is that what you think about when you miss me, Margaret Moore?* And I blushed and laughed and tried to tell him all it meant, and he kissed me, and I forgot.

We kept our secret, because his father was strict; because his mother had her moods. I saw the way the warm deep of his eyes shaded flat when he talked about his father. It was a burden that held him down—his family name, and living up to it. Pleasing his father, and closing away who he really was: who he was when he was with me. He told me he wanted to be an explorer, and when I asked him what was left to explore, he said, *Everything, Mar.* He wanted to sail around the world, single-handed. He wanted to live in Egypt and look for lost treasure. He wanted it with all of him, the same way I wanted to write words that would whisper to girls like me decades and decades after I had died. And I read to him:

Futile - the winds -
To a Heart in port -
Done with the Compass -
Done with the Chart!

He didn't laugh when I read that stanza. He said, *Futile, the winds*, and I knew he saw his father's shining office tower at the very heart of Chicago, looking down on everyone. Suits and ties. A marriage made of thin silk threads and nights spent apart. The hush of a house too big for comfort. A beautiful gold-barred cage, when he wanted to swing from a mast in the deadly grasp of the Roaring Forties, navigating by the stars alone, with his always-trimmed hair growing loose and wild.

We were a secret. We were all that was real in his whole world. We were light in the dark and summer in winter and ourselves, ourselves, ourselves. And I read to him, with sunset and shadows beckoning:

Rowing in Eden -
Ah - the Sea!
Might I but moor - tonight -
In thee!

He said, *Mar, this summer—can it be ours? Still a secret, so no one can take it away from us. Ours alone.*

I said yes, because I loved him. I said yes, because he loved me.

Why would I ever say anything else?

THE DRIFTING

NISREEN SAYS, "NO ONE ever falls in love and doesn't mean it."

We are out in a wherry. Fifteen hundred hours, the last class of the day, with the sun bearing down hard enough to bleed the lake dry. Flor rows and Nisreen holds the rudder-oar and I sit in the bow. They would never let us out three in a boat, especially since that boy died, but today it is so hot no one cares about anything at all. The ensign sits under a tree with his jaw hanging slack and a wet cloth around his neck. It is too hot even for the flies to move when we swat at them, and they crush and die under Flor's hands. She doesn't row: she only pretends, every minute or so, sweeping an oar across the water, pulling us in lazy crooked circles.

Flor says, "People do that all the time. Fall in love, fall out of love. Not everything is meant to last."

Nisreen sighs. She has her hands on the oar, but there is nothing to steer. "But—that's not what they mean to happen. No one falls in love and thinks it's for only a summer."

Flor pulls the oars in and lays them across the boat. She turns so she is sitting across it, too, and lies down on the seat and lets her head tip back over the water.

"Deck Five," the ensign half-shouts. "Flor. You know better." The words die on the air.

I sit back, too, and stare up at the sun. This is a moment that stands still. But these moments, where it seems a second will last forever—these are the moments when time slips the fastest. We are already fifty summers from now, looking back.

"I mean," says Nisreen, and she is talking to herself more than to us. "With Rose. She doesn't mean for it not to last. She thinks, every time, this boy is something, and this love is real."

I almost say, *It isn't love,* but the words bite back before they find my tongue. *It isn't love,* because I know so much; because I judge so well what is love and what is nothing.

Flor says, "It isn't love. Even Rose would tell you that. Look at her—she never speaks to them. She doesn't want a boy. She wants to imagine."

"Someday, though," says Nisreen. "Maybe it will be."

Flor throws an arm back and crooks her elbow so her hand drags in the water. "Maybe it won't," she says. "We're not here to fall in love. We're here to be us. It's summer camp. It's not real."

I feel Nisreen pull back. She says, a heavy moment later, "It's the realest thing there is."

"Oh, come on, Nisreen." Flor sits up. "I don't mean us."

Nisreen says nothing. She stirs her oar through the water and the boat groans to starboard.

"And anyway—what do you think will happen in August? We'll leave. We'll be—not us anymore."

"Don't," says Nisreen.

"It's the truth." Flor's voice is hard but not from hate. From the opposite, I think: she loves Nisreen so fierce it takes my breath away. But Nisreen lingers the way Flor can't; the way Flor isn't allowed. "What, do you think we'll run away together? You want to come to Venezuela? You think my father—you think they want me to bring home some stranger-girl from the other side of the world?"

"No," says Nisreen, and there is pain in her words.

"I'll marry a boy whose father is friends with my father," says Flor. It lines up as neat as every honor on her ribbon-rack. "He'll wear a uniform, and I'll wear a white veil, and we'll have sons, and I'll never see them because they'll be in boarding school all year and at Marshall in the summer, and they'll grow up and wear uniforms too. And I will never be in love and that's the way it is."

"What if—" says Nisreen, and the wherry creaks and lists. She is leaning closer to Flor now. "What if it didn't have to be?"

And Flor is turning away; turning back; and before she can answer the shore bursts out in shouts loud enough to send ripples through the heat.

We look. I say, *Celestial Nav,* because there is Rose on the beach with a cousin, a Deck Two girl, and there is the rest of the class bursting out of the Naval Building. The boys are in the water already, grabbing the last wherries, rowing hard into the heat. The girls wade in after them. Rose and her cousin flip the last boat and fit the oars into the locks.

"Watch out," Flor mutters, hiding away from her words. "If she's on the way out here to get us to practice semaphores—"

We are laughing still, grateful for it, when the wherry sidles up next to ours.

"What?" Rose asks, abrupt, and we shut us up and say it's nothing. "Good," she says, "because look at that."

She points. We squint into the glare.

"God," says Flor. "Not another boy already."

"Not another one," says Rose. "The same. Out on the Island."

Two boys are clambering up onto the old wooden raft—three boys now. Off past it, two wherries float unmoored with second classmen manning them. The boys on the Island are laughing and all in white.

"I'm going," says Rose. "To meet him on the Island. He asked me."

"How romantic," says Flor.

"Stop! It *is*," Rose insists. Her cousin sighs, world-weary. "Anyway," she says, "follow me, all right? Not too close, but close enough, so you can see and tell me what he thinks—"

"Rose," says Flor. "You're not honestly going to do this."

"Flor," she says. "I honestly am. It's our last summer. I'm tired of being—Rose Winston, the UC and the code-flags girl and—*Rose Winston can sail in no wind*—"

"But you can," says her cousin, jealous.

"But I want them to *see* me," says Rose. "What if I go all the way through every Marshall summer and I never once kissed anyone, never walked along the lakeshore path and hid on that point—"

"Good," says Flor. "You're too smart for all of that anyway."

"I'm not just *smart*," says Rose. "I can be a girl someone likes. Someone who looks at me like—like—"

Her cheeks turn pink with pride or shame or both.

"It's our last summer," she says, instead. "I want to dance with a boy who isn't—some friend. I want to kiss a boy. I'm *going* to kiss a boy."

She digs both oars into the water and pulls back hard.

I want to say, *Not him. Any boy but him.* But I can't, not with her cousin here; not with all of us out in the wide-open water.

It is my fault, for keeping secrets. For keeping myself from them.

"Well, let's go," says Flor. She blows a strand of hair off her face and it falls back again and sticks to the sweat. "Do you think she'll talk to him?"

I would say no, any other time, because Rose's boys aren't for talking. They are for starry-eyed gazing and long spinning monologues about what makes them wonderful. When she comes too close, when they turn too real, the charm all falls away and she doesn't love them anymore.

But this time is different, she said. And it is: not because the boy is special, but because she has made up her mind. She is the same Rose who keeps us out so late practicing that we have to sprint the lakeshore path to make it home by taps. The same Rose who has notes scattered all through next fall's play, and a whole long list of every college where she will apply.

This time is different because she will make it so.

I feel sick again; delirious.

Flor is rowing, jabbing the oars into the water with sharp angry strokes, and Nisreen holds us steady, and we don't speak. Those last words they said before the class came barreling out—those words still float on the water, unforgotten.

And I will never be in love and that's the way it is, says Flor, in the lap of the oars and the pull of our wherry toward the Island.

What if—says Nisreen, *what if it didn't have to be?*

They are in love. I know it with all my heart. It is a real love and a true love, a love so rare and perfect most of us will never know it. It is a love that will never come again once summer is over.

It is a sin to lose a love so perfect.

It is a pain as real as the heat between us. A wound that Flor jabs into, deeper with each stroke of the oars. Nisreen holds us fast and drives them toward the future they cannot avoid; Flor leans hard into it, her back to where we are going.

They are driving toward their end and I can't stand to see them fall apart.

They are driving toward their end and watching Rose poke at love like it is an experiment; win it like it is a regatta.

She will make him hers.

Rose Winston can sail in no wind. And there is no wind today, there is no love between her and that boy, but what does it matter? She is a Winston.

She is good enough for him, the way I was not.

And the furious force of what we were means nothing at all:

Futile - the winds -
To a Heart in port -

I thought we were the port; I thought we were the anchor in the storm. But we were the wind and his family was the world.

"I think," says Nisreen, and it is faint, "she should try. To be happy."

Flor digs into the water. The Island pulls closer, shimmering in the heat. "Happy," she says, heaving the word out. "She should be. A Winston and a VanLandingham—the stars have *aligned*—"

"Stop," says Nisreen. "She isn't thinking of their names."

"Everyone else will." Flor tugs the oars again. Ahead of us, glistening, three boys stand in a row on the Island.

The boy, the Naval One boy, has his hands behind his head with his elbows out as though he is lying back on the grass. They are wet from the lake, all three of them. Their nametags wink in the relentless light. They are watching our two wherries row closer, slow in the heat. They are looking at Rose. She keeps her eyes set on some point back on the shore. I follow her gaze and it leads to the top of the Naval Building—to the code-flags on the roof. Today they spell *Golf Zulu One.* It means *All persons lost.* But it is something else, too, I think. Some secret message, like Flor sends to Nisreen when they practice alone.

On the Island, the Naval One boy says something low and conspiring, and the other two laugh hard enough that the raft bobs on the water. And he pushes them both, one with each hand, and they laugh more, and they step back and leap blind into the lake. Water flies. They swim away again, lazy, sliding through the blue-green to the wherries.

He stands alone on the Island. Even soaked and sunny he is perfect: he is a knight in shining gold; he is a prince looking over his realm. He is a conqueror watching as Rose pulls for him. She is fifty feet off now and pausing. Letting her hair out and combing the curls with her fingers. She is off at our port side, and we are drifting wide, and Flor lets her arms go slack, too.

Rose turns, finally, with the oars propped on her knees and her thumbs smoothing at her eyebrows.

She looks at me, right into my eyes, and there is hope and light and life there.

Nisreen said, *No one falls in love and doesn't mean it.*

It is not Rose's fault that Flor and Nisreen will end with the summer; it is not her fault that she wants to know what love is, or that she is so hungry for it—to be a girl instead of a Winston. It is not her fault that she has chosen the boy who threw me away.

I love you, Mar, he said in starlight on the shore.

I am spinning in heat that buzzes and clings to my skin. The cicadas scream from the green, in the thick of the trees where Butterflies are bursting out from the woodland path, where they are chanting their cabin marching-song: *Five, Five, Cabin Five, we are the best girls alive.* I am spinning in the heat, and the world is glare and buzz, and I am swinging my legs up and over the bow with my saddle-shoes tied tight. I am grabbing with both hands on the white-painted wood, and pulling splinters into my skin, and I am balanced there with the boat listing.

I let go and plunge in.

I am swimming, hand over hand, with my blouse and my boat shorts dragging in the water. I am swimming, hand over hand, through the shine of the lake. I am grabbing the ladder and it is burning hot from the sun. I am finding the bottom rung, down in the cold and slick with moss. I am climbing up, I am pulling myself onto the Island where I have never stood before.

I am climbing up, and I am here, and he is here—

THE ISLAND

WE ARE A PHOTOGRAPH seared into time by the flash of the sun.

We are a boy and a girl on a wooden raft. The paint is peeling, curling back to show the old colors. The spaces between the planks could swallow me up and drop me down into the water. *The deepest spot in the lake,* they told us our third-class summer. *It's right out past the Island. The ground drops away, ninety-nine feet down into the dark, and so still if you dropped your nametag in the water it would sink straight to the bottom. It would sink all the way down, and land in the mud, and never wash away.*

We are a boy and a girl on a wooden raft, floating on the lake I love. We are face-to-face for the first time since the storm, and we are here at the very edge of Marshall Summer Naval School, and on one side of us is home and comfort and drifting white-wood boats, and on the other side is the wide open lake and the dead drop of the floor falling away, and the still waters run deep down to the bottom, and there buried in the mud are a hundred, a thousand, many thousand names rusting from gold to orange in the cold cold dark.

The ground drops away, the UC says, and it is our third-class summer and we are sitting straight and tall under our sycamore. *Ninety-nine feet down into the dark.* We are wide-eyed and we drink it in like milk and honey. *And so still*, says the UC, *if you dropped your nametag in the water it would sink straight to the bottom.*

He is staring at me. He is staring with his eyes locked in mine, and there is color fading from his face. We are caught here on the Island, and he cannot back away. He is circling instead, like a hand around a clock, until he is standing at high noon with the lake behind him.

It would sink all the way down, the UC says, and the light is fading, and a girl is whispering know-it-all that when the first classmen go out on the *H.H. Bedford* for the First-Class Sail they will unpin their nametags and let them fall: a hail of gold across the water. And all the gold will sink down, *and land in the mud, and never wash away.*

He is staring at me.

He is swallowing and swallowing, and he is colder than he ever was in the grip of dead December when we danced under orange streetlamps; when our breath turned to smoke in the air; when we sang tunes we couldn't carry: *Summertime, and the living is easy.* He was warmth like firelight all winter, but here in the blaze of summer he is ice and blue.

I step closer to him. I am at the center of the Island and he balances on the edge. He will not look away and he will not speak. And I step closer still, and he is right in front of me, and if I reached out my hand it would graze his wet hair.

We are a boy and a girl on a raft. We are a boy and a girl who were in love. I am close enough to touch him, and he is so very familiar—like home, like the sunporch at Shady Bluff; like his arms last summer. Every angle of his face; the pitch and fall of his shoulders; the pinch of his lips as he presses them together; the scar almost-not-there on one eyebrow, from when the boys flipped their canoe the last week of Lower Camp and he caught the lip of it against his face.

He doesn't speak. He stares as though it is impossible that he could send me away and still I would come back. As though when he ended us, he ended all of me, and I am gone forever.

I am dreaming; I am dizzy; I am—I *am* gone forever when I am in front of him.

Far away there is shouting and the sound of water.

And I take the last step between us and we are close enough for dancing. He opens his mouth and he is wordless for the first time he has ever been: a boy who always knows what to say.

I have turned him silent. I have done this. I, Margaret Moore, a girl who is meant to be broken. I am not brave like Rose or bold like Flor or strong like Nisreen. I am a poet and a dreamer and a girl who sees the good in everyone. I am here in my saddle-shoes with one toe scuffed; with the water dripping from my stained-dark boat shorts. I am here with my cheeks flaming bright from sun and loss and fury. I am here with my heart scarred but beating, and I am not backing away, and I am not afraid.

He says—

Nothing.

I am taller than I was last summer.

And I speak to him for the first time since the night of the storm.

I say:

What, did you think I would never find you?

He says:

No.

And I say:

Did you think I had forgotten?

He says:

No.

And I say:

Did you think I was afraid?

He says:

No.

I am not afraid. I hate him, I love him, I am bleeding still, but I am not afraid.

And I say:

I am here.

And I rush at him, at the boy I love, and he is in my arms, and we are falling and we are strung together again. We are falling and everything is the light of the sun and the scream of the cicadas, and the green green blue of Lake Nanweshmot, come up to grab us in its fingers, come up to pull us down and down into the cold dark deep—

THE BETRAYAL

I LOVED A BOY once, before all this, and it was summer. It is summer, it is always summer, it is that summer again.

His name is *him* and my name is *her* and together, we are *us*. And we are back at Marshall and I burst with our secrets, and we will not tell a single soul. It is ours.

It is second-class summer, our very first night, and he said to me when we met in those fleeting free moments, *Come to me after taps*. And I am down the stairs of Neverland with the M burned into my palm; I am out in the rushing night. I am a ghost on the lawn in pale moonlight, borne up with our secrets. I am throwing rocks, like we are lovers in a movie—throwing rocks at his window. I am spun in circles on the lawn and we are not afraid of them seeing us, because we are invincible. We are outside his window, standing over the spot where the ground leaps hollow, and if anyone were to look out and see us shrouded in the bright of night, they would see no one and everyone, because we are every Marshall boy and girl in all its long proud history.

We are walking through the dark together. We are climbing out to that hidden place on the shore, and he holds me steady on the steep of the bank. We are there almost until dawn, until the sky begins to glow, and it takes us too long to notice, because we ourselves glow even in the dark.

The days stack one upon the next. We have found the chapel doors ajar and inside the church is darkest black, and we climb up and I would be afraid, but I am not because it isn't me; it is us. He says on the stairs, *It's haunted, you know,* and I say, *those ghost-stories, they're not real, or they would have statues on the lawn like that girl—the girl struck by lightning.*

We are climbing up, and I am blind in the dark but he knows his way, and suddenly and all at once we are in the carillon room with the bells hanging imperial. He says to me, *Well, what if it's her ghost?* And right then there is a fluttering high in the eaves and I shriek and fall against him, and we fall into the bells: the highest bells, all in a row, and they clang out bright and he is laughing and clasping his hand over my mouth like that strange clashing melody is me and not the bells. Like I am the song breaking through the dark.

I think I am.

The days stack one upon the next and it is the Midsummer Dance, and there are lights around the drill-field and music playing late, and couples sway together and walk hand in hand, and we are still a secret. We are better than those lovers kissing out in front of everyone, until the lieutenants scold them. I tell him, breathless, when we have stolen away—

We are real and we are true. We don't need to tell them all so they can say we are in love. We only need us to be in love, and that means—we are the truest love of all.

He kisses me, and we are running up the pier to where the *H.H. Bedford* waits, back from its evening sail. The beach is empty and we are not allowed out here because we might kiss or drown, but it is worth the risk. The gangway is put up and he leaps the space and reaches for my hand and I am afraid, but I jump anyway, and he catches me. When my back is on the deck and he is looking down at me, I am looking up at the endless sky and thinking of all the places in the world we could be, someday, under stars and sails and dark.

The days stack one upon the next.

I belong to him and he belongs to me, and it is ours alone.

But there are rumors that spread like rot. I won't believe them, because they are lies, and of course people talk about him, because he is a VanLandingham. I would never believe them when I could believe him instead—the boy who has told me his secrets; the boy who knows every inch of me; the boy who can whisper those poems back to me now: *Wild nights - Wild nights! Were I with thee—*

Until all at once I am hit with the truth.

Until we are on permit, a Sunday afternoon. We are traipsing up the woodland path, my girls and me, to the root beer stand, and all day the dread has been stirring deep within me, because there are too many stories to sing all of them away.

Until we are crossing back over North Shore Drive and there, screaming around the curve, comes a shining bright car. And everyone at the root beer stand is shouting, and a man on the sidewalk grabs for Nisreen, lagging slow behind Rose and Flor. I am farther back still and daydreaming, and I stop dead in the road and the car barrels straight at me and the tires squeal and then, with a great roar, it swerves and jumps the curb and crashes against the wall.

I am standing untouched and alone in the road, and cars honk and the sidewalk-man rushes to see if I am all right, and Deck Five is falling over the railing and off the low wall, shrieking my name—

and I am untouched and alone with not one scratch

and they are saying all around me, *it's a miracle*

and I am staring at the car that missed me by three feet

and I am staring at the boy behind the wheel

and I am staring at the girl in the passenger seat

and he is climbing out and for one moment, one last moment, hope is that thing with feathers, and I think he will say, *Mar, Mar*—and take me into his arms

and the girl from the car is crying out his name

and he says *Rebecca, thank God you're all right*

and he takes her into his arms

and he kisses her for all the world to see

and they are pulling me in, my Deck Five girls I betrayed for him

and they are saying *she's in shock*

and he is holding her paper-doll hand, her summer-sundress hand

and I know why he never took me home to that grand old Victorian

and I know why he never danced with me when anyone was watching

and I am sick

I am sick

THE DROWNING

WE ARE IN THE watercolor.

Down here beneath the surface it is cold and still and silent. We are spinning through the water, slow and dreaming. The light streams down in mute broken beams like it does through the glass in the chapel.

We will float. It is what they tell us, the first week of Butterflies, for the girls who are afraid of water. We will float up to the air, and even if we can't swim, we can wait on our backs on top of the water, to be saved.

We will float but today, for a long tempting moment, we sink instead, strung together like chains against each other's limbs. I keep my grip where my fingers press into him. I watch the air bubble up from our mouths, so desperately alive that it is enough to make me want to argue back: to let out my breath and sink to the bottom. To feel my toes push through the gold names rising from the deepest-down place in the lake.

We sink, strung together in the silence, and I am not afraid.

And then all at once he is fighting. All at once he is that proud VanLandingham boy: the boy with that lakehouse girl in his car every permit weekend, a tall girl with bright dresses and hair that curls around her face and frames it like a portrait. She is pretty and perfect and she is his. She is kind, I think, or at least well-mannered: a girl grandmothers smile at for her grace and her modesty. I am no one to her not because she is cruel, but because she does not know I am alive. She does not know that the girl her boy nearly killed with his car is the girl he killed anyway, when I saw him for what he was.

He is fighting now. He is kicking to break the tangle of my ankles. He is clawing where my arms lock his against his torso. And I will not try to kill us; I will not try to drown him. It is only that I am not ready to float. It is safe here in the watercolor, where he flails and still is graceful, and where he shouts but his words turn to air.

He is fighting now, for his life, and I love him and hate him, and I will not let go.

And I will not try to kill us.

I will not try to drown him.

I only want to stay one more moment here where all the world is water and sunbeam and silence.

He screams. Loud enough, clear enough, that I hear the word even through the water.

Mar—!

I let him go.

THE SURFACE

HE BURSTS INTO THE bright. He is coughing and thrashing, and cursing and pale. He is dragging himself up the ladder with his feet slipping on the rungs, and he is collapsing on the burned-blue paint, and he is flat on his back with his chest heaving. He coughs up lakewater and fear.

I float.

I am weightless on the warm bed of the water a little distance away, filled up with a peace so whole I am drunk on it.

Off on the Marshall side of the Island, his boys call, *What the hell, what happened.* My girls drift closer to each other and farther from the Island.

He sits up, breathing hard enough to rock the raft.

Damn, says his second-class boy in the idling wherry. *Thought you could swim better than that.*

His chin comes up and he shouts, hoarse and terrified, *It's not a damn joke, it's not a JOKE.* He staggers up to one knee, and he leans over, and then he is retching into the lake, and staying there, bracing, with his chest rising and falling too hard.

Sorry, sorry, says the second-class boy. Past the Island I see a streak of white paint, and the wherry slides up along it and the second-class boy grabs hold.

I float. I drift out past where they will let us, and the lake is as smooth as I have ever seen: smoother than any glassy night, here at the bright peak of afternoon when the wind should gust and gust.

Didn't you see what happened? he asks, and they are far away now.

I wasn't watching, says the second-class boy, ashamed.

God damn, wasn't anybody? What about—where the hell was the ensign, I could've drowned, he says.

There is a smile on my face. I can feel it in the way the sunlight lands. I am perfectly perfectly fine, and he is almost dead.

It's too hot, says the second-class boy, feeble. Off away from them, Rose and her cousin and Flor and Nisreen have swung up alongside each other and they are murmuring with their heads down, and the water pulls them farther from the Island, even without the slightest breath of breeze.

*This—after what happened the second week—*says the boy who said he loved me. *One of us dies, and—and—*

I float, I float, I drift out toward the deeper blue. I think I am there now, over the place where we will drop our nametags. And I think of all those names in the mud, growing alive with lilting strands of moss, and caught in time. My father's name next to that boy's grandfather next to Rose's uncle, the one who died at war on a Navy ship. Names and names, and the letters fade, so *VanLandingham* and *Winston* and *Moore* are all the same.

I didn't see, the second-class boy says, and he is so far away it is like he is in a dream, or I am. *Nobody saw anything.*

I am smiling at the sun.

Well—says the boy who took me up and cast me down—

Well, let's go back to the shore—let's get the hell off this raft, he says. He is climbing down into the wherry, and his hand on the ladder grips too hard.

He will not tell the truth.

He will keep our secret, and it will be a little more real because it is only ours.

They are pulling away. He is rowing hard to steady himself. He is finding me where I float and he sees me glowing in the light; he sees that I am not afraid. He sees that I did not try to kill us. I did not try to drown him. I only held him in my arms, the way he held me once.

I float. I close my eyes, and still I smile, and in my head is the poem I love more than any of those others now. Last summer dripped with love-songs, but there is more beneath them, hanging underwater where the green fades down to black.

I float. And I say to myself, and not to him:

And do I smile, such cordial light
Opon the Valley glow -
It is as a Vesuvian face
Had let its pleasure through -

I turn for the shore. I swim for my girls.

THE CALM

WE DON'T SPEAK ON the walk back along the lakeshore path. We don't speak at all, but Rose is strung tight with worry and Nisreen's eyes are large and Flor snaps at every third-class girl who bothers her with questions. *Flor, Flor, are we in our shorts or our kilts, are we bringing our things for the kick-ball game, what time is—*

"It's supper," she says. "It's a thousand weeks into summer, and if you still need to ask me, go downstairs and knock on the office door and tell them you want to join Deck Six—"

The girls grumble away: *It was only a question.*

And she says, slapping the gold M so hard I can feel it sting my palm: *It was only an answer.*

We will tell no one.

We have a secret that is ours now, and it wraps me like relief. We are lining up with our eyes straight ahead. The summer has shifted and turned darker.

After supper we practice code-flags and semaphores. We are one: the whole great *us* of the Deck. It is not long until the Victory Race now, and we will be ready. We will prove it, to all of them, that nothing will keep us down. We have found buckets of orange paint in the art-room—a second-class girl who paints pictures so real and yet so unreal it twists me to look at them, of the trees on the shore and the sailboats in sunset light. We have spilled the paint across the sidewalk outside the doors to Neverland, and it is bright orange now, and the soles of our shoes are tinged too.

Tonight there is not one boy out on the lake.

Tonight we are Deck Five: we are girls. We are flags slashing through the coming dusk, writing words only we understand. We are a nest of secrets and truth. We are our very own world.

It is glorious.

PART II

SUBIMAGO

THE TELLING

THE HEAT SWELLS BROAD and unforgiving. It hasn't rained a single day in ages: not since the storm that caught us on the shore of Shady Bluff. The grass bleaches out to an ornery brown. One spark from a match, dropped careless, and we will all explode in flame.

Before, the nights were cold even when the daytime heat soared. But now the air is hot and bloated. We shove the window as wide as it will go, point fans straight at our faces, and still the sweat drips down our skin to paint us on our sheets.

Nisreen doesn't sleep. She stirs and stirs and stands,

finally, long into the night. In the moonlight she is thinner than she was at the start of summer and her ribs catch every shadow. Along the wall, Flor sleeps fitful but deep.

Nisreen says, so soft it is almost unspoken: *We want to know the truth.*

I curl in against myself. I am better now, I think, than I have been all summer; than I have been since I betrayed them. There is still too much to unbury, but I am standing at the grave and I am not afraid.

She says, *We love you, Mar. We do.*

She says, *Last summer—*

And it is last summer and next. We are sleeping in our Butterfly cabin. We are in this room for our first-class summer. We are gone off to wherever we will go, and our names are at the bottom of the lake.

Rose talks about time when we sit where our path dead-ends in Lake Nanweshmot. She tells us time is not that hard thing we think it is. *There's a theory,* she says, and Flor will roll her eyes and start to complain, and Nisreen will say, *No, I want to hear.*

Rose will say, *Time, and space—it isn't one line. It is strings all tangled together, a million different nows happening at once, and the past hasn't happened yet, and the future is already over.*

Flor will say, *That doesn't make any sense.*

But I think it does. Not with numbers, the way Rose

means it, but with words and truth. It is like my father told me—like my father will tell me someday when I am packing for my first Butterfly summer: *This day is endless, too.*

Everything is always, and all at once. Like us here in Neverland, where we are closer to the girls who left ages ago than we are to anyone who isn't us.

I look at Nisreen where she stands by the window, and it could be last summer, when I should I have told. It could be next summer and we are gone.

I sit very still with my legs curled up to my chest.

It is last summer and next. And there is nothing to be afraid of in telling, because I have already told her everything.

I say to her: *Last summer there was a boy.*

I say to her: *Last summer I lied.*

I say to her: *He is why I had to go away—he is why I left—*

She is very still, too, but swaying, like that Butterfly from the infirmary.

She says, *The boy—the one you ran to find in the storm—*

I never told her that. She can't know it, unless Rose is right and time is strange and tangled, and the hands of a clock run slower—or faster, maybe; I can't remember—if we are caught in the gravity of something greater than ourselves.

Or unless I am right, and there is a slipping magic here

in Neverland; in being a girl. And she knows because I know.

She says, *He's the boy Rose found, isn't he?*

THE CONFRONTATION

THE STORY BLEEDS OUT, the way stories do, whether they are true or not.

There was once a girl struck by lightning, who died in a burst of light with the stars and stripes on fire above her: a story that is true. *There was once a girl who drowned herself from heartbreak, there was once a boy who went to dig at that hollow place on the field and was caught and sent out on the Cavalry trail and disappeared:* stories that are only stories. *There was once a boy who died out in a wherry, because of those Deck Five girls who shouted at him:* a story that was true before fear turned it to a lie.

There was once a boy who almost drowned out past the Island.

There is an electricity to the air today. It is breakfast, and the mess is quieter than it should be. The director stands at the door with a lieutenant, squinting west, and they are talking about a weather hold, but only if a storm comes.

We are last today in the battalion rotation, and the boys are through eating but not getting up: sitting, instead, in front of scraps, with their eyes shifting toward us girls.

We wait at the very back of the line. Rose is holding tight to the summer we want to be true: "This afternoon, if we get this weather hold," she says, "let's have semaphores and code-flags run back to Neverland so we can practice in the hall—"

We nod. Nisreen is behind Flor with her hands on Flor's collar, smoothing it where a corner pokes out, and Flor leans back and bumps into her on purpose. I wait for them, and my eyes skim across the mess to the battalion officers. He is shaken even this morning, and everyone knows he almost drowned out past the Island, and it doesn't make sense, because he is a boy who can right a scow and swing back on even in the whitest waves Lake Nanweshmot will ever see.

I can't tell if he is ashamed or afraid, or if he is angry with me.

Rose turns and says, "Aren't you *coming*?", because we are dragging behind while she rattles off her plans.

And I am lingering and coming to a stop at the end of the bat officer table.

He won't look up.

He will not let me be anyone to him.

If it were only that betrayal, I could move on from him,

I think. But there is still too much I have not let myself unbury. And now that I have pulled him down to the dark—

Now those things are clawing out of the dirt. The betrayal is only the green-brown grass that grows over the grave.

I remember the storm.

It is flickering now, in the mess, through the high-up windows.

The floor rocks like the deck of a boat and I grab at the table to steady myself. Silverware rattles on trays, and the girls' bat com looks up, and another bat officer, a Deck Three girl, is stranded in the middle of a sentence that ends with my name.

She looks at me. She says my name again, shriller. *Margaret Moore, it's because of Margaret Moore—he almost died and it was all her fault.*

"Sit down," says the girls' bat com, grabbing her arm and tugging at it, and Flor has spun away from Nisreen and she is here at my side.

Hush ripples out from where we stand.

Flor says, "What was that? I couldn't hear you screaming it at everyone."

The Deck Three girl is half out of her seat. "Margaret Moore ruined last summer. And now this summer's ruined too, and it's all because she's back—"

Flor steps between us. She is calm and threatening. "She isn't *back* any more than you are."

"But I didn't—"

"You didn't what?"

Rose and Nisreen have gathered behind Flor, and Nisreen is whispering for her not to go any further. And Flor says, calmer, "What didn't you do?"

"I didn't get kicked out," says the Deck Three girl, fidgeting with her green scarf. Across the room the director nods to Lieutenant Caldwell, and she starts across the tile.

"Neither did Mar," says Flor.

"She did, and everyone knows it. Her parents called, and she ran out into the storm, and your whole deck followed and broke all the rules and they canceled the Victory Race." The Deck Three girl is trembling. "She wrecked everything and now she's back for blood—"

The boy looks up.

It is written on his face: that he would have died yesterday if I had wanted it.

He is looking up and it is a tide rushing between us. I cannot hide from him any longer. He cannot hide from me.

The Deck Three girl says, *Shut me up. I dare you. Fight me for your traitor.* She hisses out her words, too close and gambling. Lieutenant Caldwell is halfway to us now.

Flor says, *We'll fight you in the Victory Race, and we'll win.*

Nisreen says, *Flor—let's go—let's go—*

The Deck Three girl looks between them. To Flor, wound tight; to Nisreen, with her hand against Flor's arm.

She says, *Then fight me for Nisreen. Wouldn't you be sorry if someone spooked her horse and she fell and hurt herself and got sent home—*

Don't listen to her, says Nisreen. Outside the storm is closing in, and it is last summer again, I think, but the trees writhe at the windows and it is this summer, too. It is real.

You won't, Flor tells the Deck Three girl. *But if you do, I'll hurt you worse.*

Beyond them that boy looks into my eyes and I think of all he took from me, he and his father and their name, and I think: no.

The windows shake. The Deck Three girl is smiling now. *They could kick you out for that,* she says. *You deserve to be kicked out—*

Flor says, *Sit down, Deck Three.*

Lieutenant Caldwell says, *Girls. That's QUITE enough.*

You deserve to be kicked out, the Deck Three girl says, *and Margaret Moore—*

I say, *No.* And with it, swelling through it, there is a gash of lightning, and it shatters our teeth and makes us blind, and thunder cracks so loud it has a color to it, and the lights in the mess go dead.

The silence that comes after rings out in the dark. I taste dirt and copper.

The Deck Three girl says, *She deserves—she deserves to be dead—*

THE MISTAKE

IT IS SECOND-CLASS SUMMER and he has betrayed me, the boy I trusted with my life, the boy I loved and loved and thought loved me

and I am on the road

and he is with her

and I cannot believe it and I won't, but it is true.

It is second-class summer and we are walking back along the woodland path high up above the lake, and Rose and Nisreen have their arms in mine to hold me steady, and Flor walks ahead to clear the path, and Deck Five is a swarm behind us, bearing us back home, saying, *I can't believe he almost killed you!*

and I stumble on every root

and I stub at every rock

and I think I will faint, I think I will be sick

and in the trees, in the trees, the cicadas sing so loud

and the path has never felt so endless

and I have never felt like more of a stranger to them. They think I am only stumbling because that car nearly killed me: I was in my daydreams and my poems and because I would not stop for death he kindly stopped for me in his shining car there at the bottom of the hill.

It is second-class summer and they are chattering up into the trees and it buzzes like the summer-bugs

and someone is saying, *wait—it was who? Jack VanLandingham?*

and someone is saying, *yes, and that girl—I saw them last permit, at the Lake Festival. Her family comes to chapel and sits up in the balcony with his father—*

and someone is saying, *I wonder if we'll drill tonight or practice for the Victory Race*, because they don't know, they don't know that my heart is still lying back in the road, bleeding and beating on the hot black of the pavement.

It is second-class summer and the cicadas are too loud and I am dizzy and I think I will be sick.

It is second-class summer and I am saying, *I need to tell you—there's something I need to tell you—*

It is second-class summer and the woods are a wild wild blur of green, and I am fading out to dark and dim, and far down Lake Nanweshmot shines like diamonds

and I am falling

and they carry me

and I am in the infirmary

and I am in the room where we brought Nisreen before they locked her upstairs with the ghosts

and I am in the room where they brought me after I fainted at Parade, when I was a Butterfly with the whole world ahead of me

and the nurses whisper

and it is so hot and my hair sticks to my face and I think I should sit down, but I am already sitting down, and there is dust on the white and black of my saddle-shoes

and the nurse, the one with the white hair and the same knobbed hands my grandmother has, says, *Margaret—who is the boy?*

and I say *no no, there is no boy*

and it is true, there isn't

and she says, *Margaret—who is the boy?*

and I say *no no, the car didn't hit me; I am only tired; I am so very tired and I want to go back to Neverland*, because it will be the Victory Race in three more days and we will win like we did last summer, I will be who I was last summer, before I let a boy take me in with his lies and throw me away on the street

and she says, *Margaret—who is the boy?*

and I say *no no there is no boy*

and she says, *Margaret—who is the boy who got you pregnant?*

THE HAZE

THERE IS A BRIGHT-SKIED streak through the storm. They send us running across the green with dark clouds ahead and dark clouds behind, decks and barracks hanging open, and everyone else is safe inside on our long way back to Neverland. We run; we storm furious across the green with mud and grass churning up. We are warriors with screams that shake Marshall to the core. We are first-class second-class third-class, we are banner-girls wielding flags like battering rams to crush anyone who would stand in our way.

We are, just this once, wild.

We are the girls who won the Victory Race our third-class summer.

We are the girls who scattered down the lakeshore path with the lightning all around us.

We are the girls who when one of us went out into the raging storm we all did, with the reveille bell clanging and clanging two hours past taps.

I AM MARGARET MOORE

We are the girls they broke apart last summer because one of us made a mistake and the others would not leave her behind.

We are the girls who are back, who will win again, who will be triumph and might and victory.

They will not undo us.

THE NIGHTFALL

LATE THAT EVENING, WHEN we are still trapped inside, we curl together in the room I share with Nisreen. We are all in a row on my bed. On the desk there is a pile of books: *The International Code of Signals*, and Rose's Victory Race notebook, and *The Tragedy of Hamlet, Prince of Denmark*, and *The Complete Poems of Emily Dickinson.* Flor and Nisreen are reading it now: the same precious copy I left abandoned last summer when I ran out into the storm; the book Nisreen tucked into her suitcase when the counselor came to pack my things away. This afternoon when we finished our practicing, Nisreen read aloud that poem that found me when I was floating away from the Island:

My Life had stood - a Loaded Gun -
In Corners - till a Day
The Owner passed - identified -
And carried Me away -

Rose says, in the gathering dark: *Mar, what was your secret?*

I can tell them: A *boy.*

I can tell them he betrayed me.

I can tell them I called him out into the storm, and it was futility, but I am a poet and a dreamer and a girl who sees the good in everyone.

Or I was, at least. I am not sure I am anymore, now that I am a girl who did not drown a boy, but could.

Rose says: *There has to be more.*

Flor says, knowing too much: *Maybe there isn't.*

Nisreen says nothing, the same as she did last summer when I woke in the night and flung up the screen and retched out into the dark. After, I would curl in on myself with my knees to my chest. She would peel back her sheets; she would cross the dark and sit with me and stroke my hair where the sweat molded it to my skin. And she never asked, and I never told.

I am afraid to tell. To say it out loud will write it in stone, and I will be back there in the infirmary with my secrets on the floor.

To say it out loud will bring them back down to unmake me.

Instead I look at Nisreen beside me; put my hand on hers, so she knows it should be us instead of me.

She tells them.

THE UNBURYING

ROSE SAYS, WHEN THE secrets float before us, *We'll tell, won't we?*

Last summer they wouldn't even let us ask, says Flor.

Because it's him—because they wanted to keep his stupid perfect name out of the mud, Rose whispers back with fury enough for a scream. *It makes so much sense I don't know how we didn't figure it out a thousand years ago. But if we tell them we know—*

Flor sighs and shakes her head. *What can we tell?* she asks. *Telling won't change anything.*

And Rose says, *It will change the story. It isn't fair, is it, that whenever anyone says her name, it's with a different lie underneath it, and all the while he's shaking the director's hand, and he's reg com, and every third-class girl is in love with him—*

Flor says, with her hands woven through Nisreen's, *We still don't know the things that matter. What happened in the storm—*

She breathes in, sharp and final: a wall to lock the rest of the story away, so it cannot slip in and break us apart.

Nisreen says, quiet, *We know she was with him.*

Fine, says Flor, and still the wall shines around us. *But it isn't ours to tell.*

Rose stands. She is veiled in moonlight; she is silver and restless. *We'll tell*, she says, and she is beside the desk now with her fingers on the book of poetry. *You don't have to. I know you can't, but Mar can't either, and that's the point, isn't it?*

I close my eyes—almost-close them, until only a dull glow bleeds in. I want to say, *Tell, and you will save us.* I want to say, *Tell, and it will ruin us.*

Rose says, *They've come for her like—like bloodhounds, or vultures, or—You heard those things Deck Three said, and what the boys say is worse.*

She takes three tripping steps to the door and when my eyes sliver open she is clutching at the knob with her back to us. Her shoulders hunch in, the way a Winston's never would.

I stand, too, and go after her, and take her in my arms, and the weight of last summer unspools and seeps into the floor, and I say it so soft it could be a moth fluttering between us: *He knows everything, and if we tell even a little bit—*

She stands straighter. *If we tell the part we know, he'll have to tell, won't he?* she says. *And just because he's a boy, and his father—he's only a damn VanLandingham, and I'm a Winston. I'm a damn Winston.*

Rose opens the door. Rose goes out into the hall. And Flor springs up to follow her, and they are whispering close and insistent. I stay with Nisreen; I stay and I sit down again and stare out at Lake Nanweshmot.

Their voices rise: *We'll tell.*

We can't.

We'll tell. I'll tell.

It is a chorus like the chorus of cicadas when we stand outside the mess; like the crickets out in the dark. Humming and buzzing, reflecting itself, and it is Rose's voice and it is mine, too, and I say to that boy: *I'll tell.* My stomach gnaws and gnaws.

Nisreen says, *There is more, isn't there?*

Out in the hall and on the green last summer, we say in shivering harmony: *I'll tell.*

There is the murmur of footsteps, and a curse that cuts off, and then the rap of knuckles on a door, and it is Rose Winston and all her legacy, on fire with the truth and ready to burn that boy to the ground for me.

It is all I want and it will ruin us. Not the *us* that should never have been, him and me, but the only *us* to matter.

I'll tell, and the words are on my lips, and I am on the lawn.

There is more.

The door swings open again, and Flor is there in silhouette, and she says nothing at all and we understand. We follow her out into the hall; down to the counselor's door.

In the office Rose says, *You can't tell me you haven't heard the whispers. She's a campfire story now, and he's—he's happily ever after.*

The counselor says, *Rose—*

And Rose says, *And it's only fair that he should have a consequence, too. And with everything that happened—*

The counselor says, again, *Rose. It's over. There's nothing we can do about last summer.*

Rose says, all in one swift sweep, *It was Jack VanLandingham.*

There is a pause that stretches too wide. Nisreen stares into my eyes and does not blink. Flor shakes her head, a hard twitch that could almost turn back time and undo what Rose has said.

Rose, says the counselor. *Think before you speak.*

She laughs. She laughs, Rose Winston laughs, and it is sharp and stinging with what I can't tell and can't remember. She says, *Jack VanLandingham. The damn reg com, and he's asleep in his barracks dreaming sweet dreams, and Mar—*

Flor wrenches her hand out of Nisreen's grasp; Flor grabs the knob and shoves through the door and says, *Rose!* and Nisreen is stumbling after her saying *Flor!* and I hear only what Rose said before they stormed her: *Jack Van-Landingham—*

I will not hear the rest. I will not stand in this hall where we stood last summer with the phone ringing cursed and loud; I will not let the truth claw up from beneath my feet the way it did on the dead-dark sunporch with the storm beating down.

Jack VanLandingham, said Rose. *The damn reg com, and he's asleep in his barracks—*

There is more.

There is more.

THE VISIT

I AM NOT IN love with him: not any longer. I am not the third-class girl at the campfire; I am not the second-class girl who runs across dewed grass at midnight to meet him.

I am a poet and a dreamer and a girl who sees the good in everyone.

But now I am a girl who sees the dark, too.

The door downstairs is propped open: not a rock jammed into the lock so it won't click shut, but a wooden block holding it wide enough for lakeflies to buzz in. Outside it is cold again, a chill we have not felt since June. The air settles damp on my skin.

The night is empty but I run anyway, the way I did last summer, along the lakeshore path. At every lamppost, great swarms of moths and lakeflies gather furious and dizzy, hurling themselves into the light with the soft thud of wings against glass. They hit and fall and lurch up; hit and fall again; land stunned and flopping in the grass. They are so many they dim the light. They fall into my hair and my mouth. They are many and one: a great shape that bloats and shrinks.

I am in light and then in shadow, under the oak whose branches bend across the path and dip down to kiss the lake. I am light and then shadow, and too shimmering for anyone to see me from their windows.

I am not in love with him. Not any longer. But still I run the path; still I turn off onto the Admiral's Walk and stop soundless at the gold star in front of the Legion Building to salute the Marshall dead. In the shadows there is the statue of the girl who died from lightning: gray stone mossed green, one hand outstretched, a butterfly on her fingertips. I dip my head away from her the way I always do: the way I did last summer. It is so familiar I do not have to think.

I run hand-in-hand with myself, twin girls slipping under the tall tall trees. One of us is full of hope and despair. The other is pulled smooth by all that has happened. And we are beyond the Admiral's Walk and across the drill-field; across that hollow place. We are on the grass beneath his barracks. We scrabble for pebbles, and it is the first night I stole away and the last night in the storm, and it is the night my life burst into bright flame all around me and fell in orange-lit tatters as I lay charred on the ground.

We throw stones at the second-to-last window on the third floor. We do not miss.

He is there behind the window and he knows I am here.

I will not stop until he comes out to meet me on the green place where the ground is hollow; where we can stand suspended over the dark deep truth beneath.

I dig at the dirt.

I throw stones.

He will come to me.

We throw stones—

HANNAH CAPIN

THE STONES

IT IS SECOND-CLASS SUMMER again

and there is a knife in my heart

and with every heartbeat the blood spills out of my ribs and into the crisp white of my blouse and slicks the gold of my nametag

and the blood runs down to my kilt, to my bare thighs, to my white crew socks

and the night is bright and taunting: a night like the night I first came to him

and it was not even five weeks ago, but I would not know that girl at all if I saw her here on the lawn.

It is second-class summer again and I am beneath his window.

I am not sure if I am crying. There is wet on my face, but there is no shuddering to my chest

and anyway dead girls cannot cry

and I am a dead girl

and I am throwing stones

and he comes outside and he says

Margaret

and he says *my father*

and he says *you know me, Mar, you know we could never be more than what we are—*

and I say, *but we are everything!*

and he says, *no, we are nothing*

and he says, within it, *no, you are nothing*

and I am a stupid girl, a stupid stupid girl

a poet and a dreamer and a girl who sees the good in everyone.

It is second-class summer again and he stands in front of me: a boy who took his sharp Swiss Army knife and cut his heart out and placed it in my hands.

He says, *Margaret—you knew we were only for us.*

and I say, *that was because we didn't need anyone else*

He says, *That was because we could never be anything else.*

and I say, *no, you love me*

He says, *I don't even know what love is.*

and I say, *you love me! You do!*

He says, *I don't.*

and I say, *you're lying, you're lying for your father, but you are more than that, you told me so, and I'll tell, I will—*

and he says, *Margaret—*

and he kisses me and my skin is wet against his, my lips are dead and cold, and there is blood down my shirt but he does not care at all.

There is more I want to say. There is so much more. But I am dizzy and weak and I am a stupid stupid girl and maybe I am not a girl at all anymore. Maybe I am a woman now, with all my magic drowned out of me. Now I am an empty cocoon with the butterfly shriveled and dead, its wings trapped in the cracks so it cannot fly away. A dead shell, and some molding purple-white maggot inside instead, with cloudy eyes and too-thin skin, and it is sucking out my blood and turning me sick.

He kisses me here on the drill-field, in a spot of light where the moon streams down, where anyone could see us if they looked.

He takes my hand and we are walking into the shadows of the tall tall trees.

We are walking—

No: that is wrong.

He is leading me, and I am stumbling after him under the trees and across the path to where the cannon points defiant over the water: points out at the *H.H. Bedford*, anchored on the black glass. Every mast is tall and spindling. Every spar is sharp enough to rip me apart.

He is pulling me down with him to the grass. I am saying, I think, *We have always been more.*

He is saying, *Margaret, you have always known what we are.*

He is saying, *Margaret, you have always known what you are.*

The grass is wet. The sky is black and the stars are very far away.

I say, *no no, you're lying, so he can't hurt you.*

He says, *No one can hurt me, Margaret.*

We are close to Lake Nanweshmot and here there is mud and it is crawling up my hem and staining my kilt the dark color of his eyes. The cannon points out over the lake. The tingling smell of gunpowder clings to it.

He says, *Nothing has changed.*

He is over me, and the cannon is over me, and the stars are over me, and the world is very large and very small. He is doing the same thing he has done all these nights. I have always called it, in my head, *making love,* even though the words are too jeweled and precious for our bright summer passion. Because it is frenzy and we are stupid and young and thoughtless, but we are more, and we are in love.

Tonight it is not love.

He says, *see, Mar, this is what we are.*

And I am laughing or crying: I cannot remember how to tell the difference.

I say, *You want to sail the world single-handed.*

He says, *What—*

I say, *You want to be an explorer.*

The cannon gleams in starlight.

He is sitting back now. Zipping his shorts, and they are still perfect white, and my kilt is stained with mud, and there is the knife in my chest.

He says nothing at all.

He is looking out over the lake, to where the *H.H. Bedford* is moored.

He is looking back and he says, *Fix your skirt.*

I am lying here on my back in the mud, and far up in the sky there is the buzz of the flyby at Parade, and fainting is a gig, and I am a little Butterfly with the whole wide world before me. I have not ruined anything at all.

I say, *but this is what I am.*

He says, *What?*

He reaches down and fixes my kilt; pulls the hem back into place.

He says, *Get up, Margaret, do you want to get caught?*

I say, *I'm already caught.*

He says, *I don't have time to figure out what you're trying to say, with your poems and—all this—*

I am laughing or crying. I cannot remember how to tell the difference.

And I say to him four lines from a poem that has always been a strange dark mystery, but tonight—tonight it is clear. I say to him, and to the paling stars, and the smell of gunpowder is all around me:

My Life had stood - a Loaded Gun -
In Corners - till a Day
The Owner passed - identified -
And carried Me away -

The smell of gunpowder. The sound of starlight. The blade of a knife in my heart.

I have always known what I am.

THE DESERTER

HE DOES NOT COME out of the barracks.

When I run out of stones to throw, when my fingertips bleed from it, I walk away. I cross the drill-field and pass beneath the trees. I cross the lakeshore path. The water is low and stinks of rot.

The cannon is exactly where it was last summer; where it has always been.

I sit down on the axle and trace one hand along the barrel. Tonight there is barely the starlight to catch on the uneven places.

There is a girl beneath my feet. A girl lying on her back in the mud with her kilt snarled at her waist and her underwear around her ankles. Her hair is tangled; her hair is salted with sweat. Her face is salted with tears. There is a strange smile on her face: a smile that is not a smile at all. A boy has told her, *Fix your skirt*; a boy has told her, *Get up, Margaret.* She is staring up at me, and at the cannon, and at the stars.

A boy has told her, *You have always known what you are.*

A boy found her a summer ago, almost to the day. He took her in with his kiss on the lakeshore path while the fireflies burst into flame around them; he all that winter wove a story made of truth and lies, and they were spun so close together they were impossible to unweave. He told her he loved her. He told her things he told no one else, because she was the only one he could trust, because she was the only one he loved—

No: that is wrong.

She was the only one he could trust because she was nothing. Not like that tall gracious girl with the parlor smile; that debutante-girl who kisses with her mouth closed and keeps her ankles crossed; that girl who does not know she is not the only one; that girl who is not to blame in this at all.

It is the girl here in the mud who is to blame. A poet and a dreamer and a girl who sees the good in everyone, even herself. A girl who does not see that a boy like him will serve only himself; that he will escape to her but never escape his fortune.

He will not sail the world single-handed.

He will not bring her with him when he tramps up Kilimanjaro. When he learns the tango in Argentina it will be with someone else. When he kisses someone in the fireglow sunset on some South Pacific island it will be a girl who kisses with her mouth closed and keeps her ankles crossed until there is a diamond on her finger.

There is a girl here in the mud looking up at the sky. The boy has left her here.

She has not told him what the infirmary nurse said.

She has not told him anything she wanted to say.

She has not told him not to lead her down to the mud beneath the cannon where the tang of gunpowder will fill her nose and her eyes and her lungs while she lies on her back and lets him use her the way he has used her all these long lovely months.

She is here in the mud looking up at the sky.

She does not care who finds her.

She is here in the mud looking up at the sky. She is off on the field in her Butterfly sash, looking up at the buzz of the [illegible]by. She stands waist-deep in the water with all her Deck Five sisters, victorious.

Tonight I sit on the axle of the cannon with my hand on the barrel and my eyes on the water.

There is a girl beneath my feet. She is lying on her back in the mud.

There is a girl above me with her hand on the barrel.

There is the burn of smoke and the low glowing echo of cannon-fire.

She is a loaded gun.

THE CAPTURE

IT IS DEAD NIGHT when the door swings open. In the fog I cannot remember what is wrong; cannot remember why my fingers ache and bleed; cannot remember coming home to Neverland.

The door swings open and the lights in the hall flicker green and slide across my bed and then. Then the door is open wide. Then there is light buzzing into the room, and there is Nisreen alone tonight beneath a stiff-starched sheet, and she is fast asleep and beautiful.

There is Rose at the door with fear in her eyes and she says, *Get up, get up.*

There is Flor behind her, against the wall, standing at attention.

There is Lieutenant Caldwell coming out through their door and she says, *Miss Gómez, I expected better from you.*

And there is a knife in her hand.

THE LOSS

IN THE MORNING NISREEN is gone.

Flor makes the bed with furious grief. She pulls the corners so tight they strain. She tucks the wool blanket so smooth it looks new.

She has told us everything. How Lieutenant Caldwell dragged her out and stood her in the hall and tore the room apart. How she woke the counselor and brought Flor into the office; how even after they shut us out Nisreen pushed through the door and said, *No, she never threatened her, I swear it. You can't send her away.* How they gigged the deck and stripped Flor's rank; how they called the director right then at oh-two-hundred hours, and Flor's father after that.

How Flor stood through it, implacable, and said only *Ma'am, yes, ma'am.*

How Nisreen's face washed pale like she could see it there in front of her—those words Flor breathed to life out on the water, about the end of them.

How when it was done, the lieutenant made them salute: Flor in her crooked robe, grabbed off the tile; Nisreen in her thin slip of a nightgown; both of them with knotted hair and bare feet.

How Nisreen presented arms and said, *Ma'am, first*

classman Nisreen Al-Shayab requesting permission to leave the room, ma'am, and the lieutenant said, *You have permission,* and Nisreen's hand came down and then all of her came down, into a heap on the floor, and they took her away to the infirmary.

Rose stands in the door as we stare at the space where Nisreen should be. She says, "They won't send you home. It's a pocket knife from Butterflies. Every goddamn Marshall girl has one."

Flor says, with her wet hair braided tight, "Every Marshall girl didn't threaten Deck Three."

Outside girls shuffle back from the bathroom, calling out for extra crew-socks, but it is muted. They already know.

"Neither did you. Not really. Just because Caroline Schneider from Deck Three told a lie—why would they even *listen* to her, when everyone at the whole bat officer table heard her screaming about how she'd spook Nisreen's horse—"

She paces to the window. It is gray today, and ominous: not of another storm, but of something with a deeper greater weight. "Maybe that's what we can do—talk to the bat officers. There's another Deck Three girl, but there's a Deck One and she'll tell the truth. And the boys—Daniel Garza from Troop won't lie, or Will O'Connor from Naval Five, or—"

She stops and goes still.

"Or who?" says Flor. Her eyes are on me; on where I stand caught against my desk, my hand clutching at the poetry we read last night before they broke into this place.

Rose turns. It is written on her face, the same as Flor's.

I say it: *Jack VanLandingham.*

Flor crosses to the door and shuts it hard and stands with her back against it.

"It was never Deck Three," says Rose, hushed cold. "It was him—and you know he stood there saluting and told them anything he could to get us sent home—he knows he won't get away with it as long as we're here, and he knows Mar could never keep it all a secret—"

A breeze pushes into the room and fills the air too full.

Flor says, "It won't do anything to talk to Deck One or Troop. We can't trust them, if he's talked to them."

"But Naval Five is our brother deck," says Rose. "And my cousin is Deck Two—"

"Who would go against him?" Flor's voice rings raw. "I lost my rank because of him, and they called my father. If they send me home—"

"They can't," says Rose.

"But if they do."

The reveille girl rings the bell far down the hall. *Deck Five, five minutes 'til lineup,* she shouts, and she is running closer, and the bell clangs louder until she jolts to a stop outside our door and stops her shouting.

"Deck Five," says Rose. "We can trust Deck Five."

It is true. Even the third classman who shrieked and whined when the counselor said *no phone at all, except on Saturday night*, would never turn against the deck. She has hardened into one of us now: she rows on the crew-boat and shows off her callouses, won by skin ripped open and grown stronger.

"Deck Five," Flor says, and it is a vow. She takes the books on my desk and drops them into the top drawer. She stays beside me: steadfast to the end. "No one else."

It has always been the truth.

THE DEPARTING

BUT WE CANNOT STOP our days just because Nisreen is locked up with her heart in pieces, and Flor is impassive but shattered beneath it, and all because a boy who loved me once had to go and blame us for things we never did.

We line up for roll-call and march to the mess.

It is Saturday: I don't realize it until Flor tells us, at breakfast, that inspection is at eleven hundred hours. But it is, and when we stand at parade rest in the hall, the space where Nisreen should be makes the blood rush in my ears.

"We'll go see her," Rose says, after. We stand off in the corner of the lounge, watching girls collect their permit slips at the desk. "We don't have anywhere better to go."

It is a lie. Anywhere on the whole lake is better than the infirmary. Rose has her parents' lakehouse and her grandparents', too. Or we could go into town: sit at the beach or drink milkshakes at the root beer stand or wait two hours for a table at Papa's Pizza.

"The infirmary," says Rose. "We'll break her out."

Flor pretends to smile but it is obedient and nothing like the wide open laugh-smile she gives us when we are alone. I don't understand it all, but I understand a part of it, because love wrenched away is always a little bit the same, no matter what it is that has done the breaking.

We get in the permit line and Rose digs for our slips. Flor is chewing at her cheek, and anyone who didn't know her would miss it and think she was bored: that she never stood toe to toe with a Deck Three girl; that a lieutenant never found her knife and held it like a gun; that Nisreen never went away at all.

But she is chewing and chewing, and Nisreen is gone, and today we will get her back for Flor.

"I'm sorry, girls. Flor has other arrangements this afternoon," says the woman at the desk. Her fingers smooth the edges of the permit slips; Flor's sits to the side, inked with stars. The woman is not our Deck Five counselor: she is a lieutenant from the military staff, the one who looks at Lieutenant Caldwell like a dog looks at the owner who has kicked it.

"What do you mean?" Rose asks, impetuous. "And where's Miss—"

"They're waiting for her at the gates," says the lieutenant.

My eyes linger on Flor. She is unimpressed and impossible to hurt.

"You heard that, right, Flor?" the lieutenant says. I want to be angry with her for what they did to Flor and Nisreen, but it was not her fault, and her eyes are shadowed with uncertainty. "Dress A's and take your permit slip."

We go with her as far as we can. Everything is off-balance without Nisreen: three hands hitting the gold M; three pairs of saddle-shoes on the path; three of us walking up to the gates together, instead of the four we always are. All around us there is cheer and laughter and the day is bright, but we are too stricken to talk.

We hang suspended at the last corner under a tree. A dark car idles beyond the gate.

"I don't know—" says Flor, all in a rush and quiet, and Rose and I take her up in our arms. She breathes in and out. She does not cry. "I don't know what they told him. I don't know who he sent—" And she trails into a curse. "I don't know who they talked to. If they only said I'm rank-stripped, or—that I made a threat—"

She laughs. She laughs with all the same spirit as she did in the water off Shady Bluff, but it is starred and breaking. "He'll bring me home to make it right with Marshall, and to fix the mark I put on our name. I'll never see her again and I love her, you know I do—"

And she pushes us away and stands alone. She looks so very much like she always does that it brings tears into my eyes for her: for this girl who will not cry. She is bored and lovely; she is haughty; she is dangerous; she is the general's daughter.

She takes a step backward, into the sun.

She says, "My father is a good man. He is loyal to his party. He is loyal to my mother. He will do everything he can to make the country better—he will do everything he can to raise my brother and me so we can live anywhere we want, if the time comes—"

She takes another step back. "There are people back home who can't get out—"

She takes one last step, and she is onto the walk now, and whoever her father sent can see her there, proud and nonchalant.

"My father is a good man," she says. "I am loyal to my family—"

Her voice begins to crack.

She says, "Tell Nisreen—"

Then she has turned her back, as sharp as marching,

and a door opens and shuts, and the car pulls away from the gate and leaves her last words unsaid.

THE VISIT

THEY WILL NOT LET us in to see Nisreen.

I hang back, still half on the stoop. I hate this place so much I can feel it in my throat. The nurse is the same nurse from last summer, who said, *Margaret—who is the boy?* I will not look her in the eye.

"You can't be serious," says Rose. "She isn't *contagious.* She's had her damn heart broken."

"Rose," says the nurse: Rose has never been sick a day in her life, but everyone knows the Winstons. "There's no need for that language."

"There's no need to keep Nisreen locked up all alone in a haunted infirmary, either. A haunted *damn* infirmary," says Rose, smart-mouthed and defiant. "Nisreen! Hey, Nisreen! Come down here!"

Then she is breaking for the hall with the same brash assurance she has at the tiller. I will come with her on this hopeless bid for the win. We cannot leave Nisreen. I cannot let Rose go alone. And I take a step, one step across the threshold, so one saddle-shoe hovers above the tile.

The blood rushes in my ears, and the whir of wings, and they are here, I think: the lakeflies and moths, the fireflies, all scattering in my eyes. I taste medicine as thick as tar. It is second-class summer and I am here in the infirmary, and the nurse says, *Margaret, who is the boy,* and the floor sweats with ghosts.

The nurse says, *Now calm down, Margaret, there isn't any use in ripping your hair out now. You should've thought about this when you were making eyes at some boy,* and she says, *Margaret, who is the boy,* and she is calling for her assistant, and her assistant is pouring the medicine, and when she raises it to my lips the smell is so poisoned that it chokes me before I can taste it. I say I will not. They decide for me, because my voice is back on that tire-scored road in front of the root beer stand.

They push that girl into a chair that sticks to her legs.

She cries out. She swats the medicine away and it splatters against the wall and drips brown and toxic.

They hold her arms against the chair and the nurse is old but the girl is weak and she thinks she will faint again.

She says, *I won't take it*

and they say *yes you will*

and she says *no*

and they say *yes*
and she says *let me go*
and they say *take this, take this, good*
and she says nothing
and she is gone.

It is first-class summer and I am trapped here again and I think I will faint. A whole year has passed and no time at all, because still Rose swings for the stairs and still the nurse scrambles after her. She says, *Rose Winston!*, and she has Rose by the shoulder. I have not yet crossed into this spoiled place.

"What in the world—good lord, Rose," says the nurse, out of breath. "It's only a visit to the infirmary. She's resting."

Rose stands pensive and taut. I am coming undone and she is on the verge of it, I think. She has lost her control and nothing she does can wrest it back into her hands.

They are pulling us apart.

"We know what this is about, you know," says Rose. "It's not that she's sick—it's not about a pocket knife from Butterflies, either. It's the same reason our counselor is gone, isn't it? Because of what I said about Mar—"

She stops. She laughs again, the way she did last night when she spoke that boy's name and brought last summer back to drown us.

I turn my head and breathe in. The infirmary is buried

in trees, and beyond them the stone walls of the chapel rise high. The outdoor air tastes like grass and pine.

"Fine," says Rose all at once, and I look back in at her. She smiles with the fearsome ease of a woman who knows where she stands in the world. I have never seen this Rose before. But we are all different this summer, I think. This summer I almost drowned a boy, and I almost don't know why.

"Fine," says Rose. "I'll have a talk with my father about this. How does that sound?"

And she walks out the door and down the steps with all her mother's purpose, and it does not fit her yet, but it will if they push and push at her and make her find the wrong sort of power.

She is charging on, to we-don't-know-where, but then she spins abrupt and she is herself again: Rose instead of Winston. Huffing and mad with loyalty, and much too smart for their rules.

She shouts up at the window to that haunted lonely room:

"Don't worry, Nisreen, we're coming back for you!"

Behind the window there is only silence.

HANNAH CAPIN

THE COUNCIL

IT IS SECOND-CLASS SUMMER again

and my skull pounds from the tile of the infirmary floor

and I taste the tar of the medicine they poured down my throat

and it is very hot

and there is a creature inside me with its teeth gnawing at my ribs and its eyes as dark as his.

We are here in the director's office. The nurse sits with her ankles crossed beside that old oak desk and the director rests his elbows on the wood. They make me say it myself and I will not. The nurse says it instead:

Dr. Moore, Mrs. Moore—your daughter is pregnant

and my mother's hand comes up over her mouth

and my father takes off his glasses like the words will take a different shape without them, perhaps

and the director says, *now Margaret, you must tell us—who is the boy*

and I am not answering

and I am not there at all.

I am out on the field. I am lying on my back with the flyby buzzing overhead.

I am out in the dark. I am running hand in hand with a

boy I love, and we are leaping onto a ghost ship, and we are heat and light and summer and stars, and he wants to sail the world single-handed, and I want to write words made of lakewater and impossibility.

I am out on the shore. I am lying on my back in the mud.

Margaret, who is the boy:

A boy I loved.

Margaret, who is the boy:

A boy who lied.

Margaret, who is the boy:

A boy who has always known what I am.

I cannot speak when I should and I cannot stay silent when I must and I say, *Jack VanLandingham.*

It is two words I whispered in the moonbeam light of winter to trees still weighted down with verdant leaves.

Jack VanLandingham, and his father's face is gold-framed and his name is carved in stone.

Jack VanLandingham, and Margaret Moore is no one at all.

and my father says

Margaret how could you

and my mother says

she is a better girl than this

and the director says

she is exactly a girl like this

and I am.

HANNAH CAPIN

THE FEAR

FLOR DOES NOT COME back for supper.

"Where *is* she?" Rose asks, and her voice pitches up. She is in the UC's spot again, with Flor gone, and with a heavy hanging silence after the first sergeant calls *Gómez,* twice. There is not even the shirking *Infirmary, ma'am,* that there was when she called *Al-Shayab.*

No one says a single thing.

"She can't just be gone," says Rose, to the lieutenant this time.

"Rose," the lieutenant starts. She is weary, too. "March us to the mess."

Flor does not come back for Parade. The light fades faster than it did in the full of June. When the Aviation boy does his flyby I tilt my face up and up in the twilight. All around me every chin is even; every eye is straight ahead. Looking anywhere else is a gig: *count the hairs on the head in front of you,* they told us in Butterflies. *Sing camp songs, count back from one thousand by sevens. But don't move.*

All around me every chin is even and every eye is straight ahead, and I am looking up, and the plane is so small, and the sky is infinite. We here below are both at once.

After Parade, we are screaming our Deck Five hymn

when Rose finds her father in the crowd and says—*Dad, wait—*

The hymn ends and she digs out of the tunnel. I am behind her, weaving through drums and brass. Evening settles in.

"Dad!" Rose shouts again, and we come out through a Deck One throng.

He turns and smiles his easy Winston smile. "Well, Mary Rose," he says, merry and careless. "Didn't know you were UC again this week."

She looks back to where I wait.

"I'm not," she says. "It's Flor. She isn't back from permit."

"Ah." He looks back, too, at all the chatter and listening. "Not anything like—"

"No," says Rose. "Not like last summer."

"Well then," he says like he has already forgotten. "Good to see Deck Five with the Naval Banner again—"

"Dad," says Rose. There is guilt on her face when her eyes graze mine. Then she is hurrying around a brick corner with her father beside her, and I trail them with mud in my throat.

"Dad," says Rose, again, when they are almost alone: I linger behind a sycamore. "Can we speak to the director before you go?"

His chin shifts. "Why?"

Through the leaves her skin is shade and golden light.

"I can't say it out here in the open," she says, and she nods to the shouts from the quad, where lakehouse fathers reminisce; where mothers count down from three and snap photographs.

"We can't just barge in," her father says. "It's not the yacht club."

She crosses her arms. "But you *see* him at the club all the time. You play tennis—he's had dinner at the house—"

"Mary Rose, I haven't said no," he says. "Tell me what it is, and we'll see if it can wait."

"It can't," she says. She looks to me again, and the light has changed, and for a moment I can see her thirty years from now. She will see the director whenever she wants. She will have her own seat on the Marshall board. "It's Flor. She's in trouble, but it wasn't her fault. And they've got Nisreen locked up in the infirmary for saying Flor didn't do anything, and—"

She stops.

"And what? Who else?" her father asks.

This time she keeps her eyes from mine. "It's nothing to do with Margaret, Dad," she says. Her voice is high with lies and she is a girl again, nervous and telling tales the way she did when we were ten years old at Summers Rest and I broke her mother's music box. "It's about Deck Five getting a fair chance. You believe in fair chances, don't you?"

"You know I do," he says. He is smiling; she is winning him already.

"Trust me, Dad, please?" she says with that same Winston smile, and he laughs and says, *All right, then, Mary Rose.*

They are gone. For one sunlit moment the weight in my lungs lifts away. She will tell the truth, the part of it we know, and they will hear her.

Around the corner, an Aviation boy comes yelling: "Salazar! Leduc! VanLandingham! Reg officers to the parade field—"

That boy shouts back from the quad, "We're there, we're there," and his words soar over the din, and Rose is right: he has never seen a single consequence.

And Rose is wrong: they will not come for him when she tells. They will come for us instead.

The boys bloom around the brick and through the leaves. First Salazar and Leduc, Naval Three and the Black Horse Troop, with him four strides behind.

I am cloaked in green shade. I am like that statue, I think: that dead girl, the girl who died in lightning.

He stops. He turns to look at me, and the evening light pours across him, and he is everything at once: the boy who found me by the lakeshore and the boy who left me there.

I hold the words between my lips: *I'll tell.*

He says, last summer in that grand old Victorian, *Dad, she can't—*

"VanLandingham!" shouts the Naval Three boy, and they are clattering back to him. "What is it?"

He is the boy I did not kill. I am what he threw away. We are knotted together as much as we were in the bright cold below the Island when I twined my ankles in his and let the water pull us down.

There is more. It is spilling from my veins and rising in my throat.

"VanLandingham!" they call again. "Jack, what the hell—"

The light is gold and cloying. The air hangs sweet with dead flowers and blood.

He reaches out, for a swollen second, like he will take my hand: to bring me into his arms; to push me into the mud.

His hand drops. He says: "It's nothing."

He believes it, I think.

He says, "It's nothing," and this time he is himself and his eyes steal back their gleam. He turns away. He is gone.

When I have found myself again, when I have stepped around the corner, they are far across the field: three streaks of white against the deepening green.

I say to him, and it is second-class summer again: *Jack, please—*

I AM MARGARET MOORE

THE POPLARS

IT IS A HOUSE that would make anyone stop and look.

It is a grand old Victorian on the west shore, where the town unbraids into great sloping lawns for that luxurious stretch before it curls again and turns to tight-pressed bungalows. It is a gracious driveway; it is tall trees and bright spans of grass; it is a porch that circles the house and spreads wide enough for dancing. It is, outside, summer-white with dark shutters and many windows. It basks in the light of afternoon, and I should be on the rooftop hoisting code-flags, but I have abandoned us to run away with a boy, beautiful and bright.

It is, inside, a still airy chamber with high ceilings. There is a grand piano and a staircase of rich oak. There are portraits of dead VanLandinghams who built this house with money from the railroad that once pinned Marshall to Chicago and Detroit.

The railway is gone now, its tracks peeled off the west shore lawns. The depot is for Saturday night dances with girls in short dresses spilling down the walk to the beach.

The VanLandinghams are forever.

We sit in the back room. Not the parlor with the piano and not the den, off to the other side, with its wide hearth and the stain of last night's smoke. It is a room that runs the whole width of the house, with doors to the porch and windows to the lake. The breeze swirls hot and unsettled.

We are all here together: the VanLandinghams and the Moores. I wear my Dress A's and I have washed the mud away. He wears his, too, and they are still the perfect white of June.

They are saying, my parents, *we were thinking of sending her to New Hampshire—she has an aunt there,* and it is so wildly gaily trite I almost laugh at it.

His mother says *yes, yes.* She has a glaze to her eyes like I saw in the mirror when they sent me home from the infirmary. I think she has taken something, too; I think she does not know where she is. Her face is powder-dry in the August heat.

They are saying, *we'll decide, before it arrives, where it will stay.*

His mother says, *yes, yes.*

There is a monster living in my belly. It is a thing that wants to kill me; that has already begun to kill me. It cannot breathe and it cannot feel. It can only chew on my ribs and drain the color from my face and turn me hollow.

I cannot live for months and months with this piece of him inside me. I cannot have it tear itself out of me screaming and gnashing. It will have lake-black eyes and moon-pale skin and long fingers; it will sprout downy wings like a lakefly; it will buzz and buzz when it opens its toothy mouth. It will look at me and it will say: *You have always known what you are.*

My fingers claw against my skin. It lurks there, underneath.

My father is saying, *We are disappointed in Margaret. We raised her to be a girl with self-respect, a girl with propriety—*

That boy's father says, and says far back in his throat: *Well, that didn't come to pass, did it?*

They are quiet for a long moment.

My mother says, *Our children make mistakes—*

That boy's father says, *Child? She's not a child. She's a woman; you can see that as well as I can.*

They are looking at me. I think they see the monster instead, with its dull black eyes and its trembling wings.

My father says, *Now, watch your tone.*

That boy's father says, *She's a god damned woman, and I can tell you for a fact my son has never been in one bit of trouble before, and I've never heard a word about—about any summer girl.*

He says *summer* in a way that brings bile to my lips.

His mother says, with her hair neat and her ankles crossed, *He has a lovely girl he sees. Rebecca McAllister.*

His father says, *Now that's a girl who knows how to behave herself. Not a girl mincing around with her skirt rolled up high—*

My father says, *We're in this together, aren't we? I'd think we could be civil about it—*

And his father laughs and says, *Moore, this isn't Marshall days. You know damn well this doesn't need to ruin my boy's life. If it's even his, that is. Who's to say there aren't half a dozen other boys who got her on her back—*

I am going to be sick. I am going to be sick here in this grand glowing house on the wrong side of the lake. I am looking, looking past a boy who will not open his mouth to defend me. Out onto the lake and across it. Past the Island; past the still deep place where the water holds its truths.

I cannot find Shady Bluff there on the shore. I am blind from the glare: all light, all bright, all summer. But there are girls there and I know it. Four girls in cotton scraps and tangled hair. There is water flying like diamonds. There are hands woven together and dreams and secrets. Nisreen will raise horses that run faster than wind. Flor will raise sons strong enough to stand through a dozen revolutions; strong enough to be different from their father. Rose will write numbers that send astronauts to the edge of the universe.

I will write words that live long after I am buried in the ground.

His father says, *I'll tell you the truth, I didn't believe it myself when I got that call, not until I heard it out of Jack's mouth, and I'll tell you—you can bet it wasn't his idea. He's got big plans for the company, and no minx is going to come in and saddle him with a bastard so she can marry up—*

I will write words. I will write words. I am blind from the sun on the water and I am looking at that boy again, at Jack, and I do not recognize him. He will not look into my eyes. There are ten thousand things I want to tell him and they are all a watercolor blur and I say:

You want to sail the world single-handed.

His father does not hear it and he is talking still, and my father is talking, and their voices swell. My father wants to be *rational* like this is the college and he is weaving a lecture about Romans who fell; about Rome when it burned. His father wants only to rail against the girl who has trapped up his son. I am Eve and Delilah and Salome and Jezebel. I am Medusa and I have turned him to stone. And I say:

You want to be an explorer.

His mother is saying, *Please, Teddy, let's not be cruel, surely she has enough in front of her.* My mother will not look at me. She still loves me, I know, but she is disappointed and I have done the unthinkable. And it is true: I am a girl who did not think because I was dreaming and in my dreams it was only love and passion and summer and the end would never come. And I say:

You hate your father.

It is the first thing they have heard.

His father says, *Excuse me?*

I stand up and the room is unsteady beneath me, like the deck of the *H.H. Bedford* when we leaped aboard and pushed close under the stars.

I say, *Jack. You hate him. You hate what you'll become—*

He says, *Mar, don't.*

His father says, *There it is. She's trying to turn him against his own father. Is this the girl you raised her to be? A girl who turns a boy against his family—*

I say, *You loved me.*

He says, *Mar, don't be a child.*

His father says, *Child? She's a common whore.*

It hits me in the cheek like the palm of his hand. I stagger back. I knock into a table; there is a vase of hydrangeas past season and they are turning brown; the vase is falling; the vase shatters on the floor; there are brown-white blooms all on the shining wood.

My father says, *You won't speak to my daughter that way—*

His father is reaching into the pocket of his light summer blazer and pulling out a checkbook; scribbling; ripping. He says, *And here's the due she's earned.*

My father says, *We don't want your damned money.*

His father says, *It's not for you. It's to keep our name away from your daughter's mistake. Put her on a plane tomorrow. Tonight. Get her out before the rumors start. Send her to*

New Hampshire, let her find some maiden aunt to take it in. And there will never be one breath about whose child she says this is. Not one breath.

I am a loaded gun. I am a common whore. I am an empty shell with infirmary poison on my tongue and a gray-winged beast in my belly.

I say, *I don't want to keep it.*

His father says, *That's between you and your maiden aunt.*

I say, No. *I mean I need to get rid of it—I made a mistake—I didn't think, I should've thought, and he said he would be careful and it would be fine, and—I'll die if I have to keep it—*

My father says, *Margaret, it's out of the question.*

And I say, *Please, I'll go away, I'll do anything, but let me make this choice—*

And my mother says, *You have already made your choice.*

I say, and it is weak and dangerous, and it is all I have left: *I'll tell.*

He speaks, that boy speaks at last: *Dad, she can't—*

His father says to him and not to me, *She most certainly will not.*

He still holds the check. Inside me the creature is monstrous; it is hungry; it is humming and buzzing and I am on my back on the field, with the flyby overhead, and I am on my back beneath the cannon on the lakeshore.

I say, *Jack. Please.*

He says nothing at all.

THE TRUTH

I LOVED A BOY once, before all this.

I am a stupid girl.

THE ABSENCE

FLOR IS NOT BACK.

Nisreen is not back.

There is an ice-cream social on the lawn, and we should be eating and flirting. Instead we keep to ourselves because it is us against the world. We thought it was true before, that we had targets on our backs, but that was only the Victory Race and a lie about a boy in a wherry.

This is different. The secret is out now: not all of it, but enough to hurt us.

We keep to ourselves because together we are unbreakable.

I hang back at the edge of the lawn. Deck Five is a wall that keeps me safe. Deck Five in front of me, and Neverland behind, and Lake Nanweshmot on one side, and on the other is the walk toward the gates. I look down the walk, again and again, waiting for Rose to come back.

She does not come back.

We leave while the rest of Upper Camp is still licking melted sugar from their fingers and dancing in the coming dark. *They didn't have the good ice cream anyway, from the root beer stand,* says a second classman, trudging up the steps. A third classman, the one who almost cried when they took away her nail polish during move-in, says, *And all the boys in this whole camp are ugly anyway.*

It's a lie. She has stared all summer at a boy from the Black Horse Troop. But she is loyal like the girl who scoffed at the grocery-store ice cream, and like every girl coming home thirty minutes before closing. If one Deck Five girl is unwelcome, none of us stays.

Besides, we know what happened with Flor and Nisreen. We won't celebrate without them.

And Rose isn't back.

I don't ask, at taps, where she is.

She isn't gone. She is only away with her father, and

Flor is only on permit, and Nisreen is only in the infirmary, and nothing is the matter. The search was nothing at all and they know, of course they know, that every girl who was a Butterfly has a pocket knife in her desk. That girl in the mess did not know how I almost drowned a boy. We were far away in the blinding sunlight, and when we fell we were on the other side of the Island, where no one could see from the shore.

Long after taps the door swings open and Rose looks in. I follow her into the office.

She says, standing at attention, "They sent her away, didn't they?"

The lieutenant says, "Who?"

Rose says, "Flor. She said something she shouldn't have, but so did that girl from Deck Three, and she didn't get sent home—"

"No," says the lieutenant, and she is weary again. Not tired: everyone is tired this many weeks into Marshall, however many weeks it is. This is more than that, and deeper. "Who do you mean sent her away?"

Rose fidgets. She steals a glance over her shoulder, like she is asking my permission to say the rest.

I cannot tell. They will come for us if I tell. I know it as sure as I know anything at all; I know it with a fear that burns down my throat and seeps into my veins. But this will not be telling, will it? We are here in Neverland, and it is only us, and anyway, Rose does not know the things that would tear us down.

I do not say anything at all.

Rose turns back. "Whoever sent Mar away last summer."

"Rose," says the lieutenant. "Margaret's parents withdrew her early." She will not look at me, as though she can believe her lies if she doesn't see me standing where I stood last summer with sweat on my neck and my fingernails digging at my stomach.

Rose stands mired in it. Finally she says, testing the very last limit, "You'd swear on the Marshall M that Flor isn't gone, and our counselor, and it's nothing to do with Mar and Jack and what happened that night in the storm—"

"Rose," says the lieutenant. "That night—you know what happened."

"Do I?" Rose asks. "Does anyone? Or are we afraid to ask at all—"

It is coming back again: the truth I have held down beneath the water until it shook and shrieked and breathed its last.

"Will I be next?" Rose asks, far-off, and I am gasping for breath.

I remember the storm.

"Not like Mar," says Rose in echo, and I almost think she will laugh again. I almost think she will cry. I am staggering away, one hand dragging at the wall with such weight it could bring Neverland to the ground. "Like Flor and Nisreen—will they send me away in a car, too, or take me to the infirmary in the middle of the night—"

I remember the storm.

I remember how the phone rang and rang that night.

I have not spoken one word to them since the night they came to take me away.

I ache for them. For the mother who lifted me out of the watercolor and laughed and laughed; who smelled of the flowers in the garden and the cakes baking in the oven. Who left stacks of books on my nightstand, and I devoured them, and she brought more, and when I said *I want to be a poet*, she did not laugh; she said, *Then read, and read, and write.*

I ache for them. For the father who read in a haze of cigar smoke my mother hated but pretended she didn't, because she loved him; who told me stories of Greeks and Romans; gods and men; immortality. Who told me to be brave when my chin wobbled on the porch of that Butterfly cabin, and said, *Here you will become who you are.*

I have.

I made a choice and could not choose again. And I begged and begged, and said I would die, and they said only, *You are a child, you do not know what is best*, and *You are a woman, you will bear your consequences.*

I am not sure that I am either. I am not the bright pure thing they want me to be, and I am not the thrown-away girl in the mud, and I am not what that man says I am.

I am—

It does not seem that there are words for it.

I am running out into the storm and they are flying around the lakeshore.

I am here in Neverland after a whole dead year, and they have made friends with the man who called me those terrible things, and they have not come back to Shady Bluff because they are ashamed; because this one thing about me has become all that I am.

I ache with the hurt of what they think of me, but I ache with missing them too. And I think—if only I could speak to them once more, if only I could explain the way I could not last summer—then they could drive through the dark again, and it would be poetry, and I could run away from here and find my beautiful girls and we could come back, fearless and forevermore.

I am here in Neverland and there is a monster chewing up through my ribs and taking my heart into its jigsaw teeth. I am here in Neverland and I cannot speak

and I remember the storm—

HANNAH CAPIN

THE STORM

IT IS A STORM like the end of the world and it is, I think.

It is second-class summer again and I am on the green. I am in the rain and the thunder and I think of that girl, the one who died in lightning: the one who turned to stone.

There is nowhere for me to go. I have betrayed my Deck Five girls, and I have disappointed my parents, and my parents have fed me to the wolves, and the boy who loves me has left me to die. There is a monster in my belly and it is growing and they are coming for me on the black tar road. They said:

Margaret, it's time to go

and I said, *no no, let me stay*

and they said, *you have made your choice already*

and I said, *no no, it will kill me*

and they said, *Margaret, you are leaving*

and I said, *no no, there is no boy*

and I dropped the phone and fell back against the wall

and I thought I would be sick but when I bent sharp and doubled over against myself there was nothing left to let go

and I could hear them in the phone, in the walls, and their voices buzzed and buzzed and they said, *it's time to go it's time to go* and I ran out into the storm and I am running still, through the lightning, and there is a knife in my heart.

I am on the lakeshore path and I am on the green. I am falling down onto my hands and knees and digging for stones and there is nothing left, nothing but a large round rock the size of my fist.

I dig it out of the dirt. I climb up to my feet and stagger back into the full of the rain; onto a lawn that is more brown than green. I throw the rock with all my might.

A bolt of lightning comes cracking down behind me, not even fifty feet away, against that place where the ground is hollow, and it breaks through into the deep.

I think, *that girl died in this lightning.*

The rock has hit his window.

I have fallen back into the mud.

I cannot tell if I have been struck by the lightning or if it is only me but I am glowing I think. I am glowing through the mud on my shoes and the blood draining into my shirt.

And he is there in the shattered glass.

He is there in his tower with his hair dry and his uniform white and starched, and I am here in the gutter.

He is there.

He says, *Jesus Christ, Margaret.*

He has the rock in his hand. Above his head the window is spines and teeth.

He says, *You're going to die out there in the storm.*

I say, *Don't you understand, I am already dead.*

He says, *You need to go.*

I say, *Don't let them take me away, you can't let them leave me with this, when you said—*

He says, *Margaret, go back to your deck. Go to your parents—*

I say, *I'll tell! I swear I'll tell—*

And he says, *Jesus! Margaret—okay, okay—*

He is gone from the window and then he is back and pulling a raincoat onto his shoulders. He says, *Margaret—I'm coming outside—hold on—*

I should not believe him. But I am a poet and a dreamer and a girl who sees the good in everyone and anyway I have nowhere else to go.

When he comes out under the trees I am standing over the hollow place in the drill-field. I am standing in a charred black circle where the lightning burned the grass away even through the rain. There is no life here. This summer we stood in this spot and kissed with all the passion and eternity anyone could imagine, and now he is a stranger.

He says, *Margaret.*

I should not trust him.

He says, *Margaret, I'm here—I'm here*

and then he is here in the dead circle and he has his arms around me and at first I think I will scream because it is too much like that night he led me to the lakeshore before I could remember how to walk away

and then I think I will cry because I do not know how everything changed between us

and then I think I will cling to him until the storm dies, until the grass grows back, until all of this is only a terrible dream and we are third classmen again walking hand in hand and blessed with firefly light.

I am crying and my head is against his chest; against his heart. His hand is on my hair and he says, *I can fix it.*

I say, *but it's too late, and they're sending me away, and—*

He says, *Not if we run away first.*

He has my hand in his. He has taken off his raincoat and draped it onto my shoulders and it is too big, and I am drenched and sick. He is leading me across the field and toward the lakeshore path and ahead of us the cannon gleams wet. I say, because this time I remember how, *no*, but he has my hand in his and he says, *trust me, Mar.*

I should not, but there is nothing left to happen that has not happened already.

He says, *come on, we have to hurry.*

He has my hand in his.

We are running now, down the lakeshore path, and far behind us there is shouting: my name scatters across the grass. Far behind us there is the dizzy sweep of flashlights that cannot cut through the storm.

We are running down the lakeshore path and I do not know what he thinks he can do that will save us but there is nowhere else for me to turn and I am so very very tired. We are running for the Naval Building where it stands staunch and true and bright and brave with three code-flags snapping hard in the wind: *Alfa Echo Two.*

Mar, he says.

Mar, don't fade on me now.

We are on the beach. He has let go of my hand and I say, *no!*, but he is hauling a wherry across the sand and into the lake and he says again, *Margaret—*

I am frozen on the shore. The water is black and churning and the rain is so thick I can hardly see the *H.H. Bedford* at her mooring.

He steps out of the boat. He grabs my hands and he says, *Margaret. We'll get away from them, and then—we'll fix this.*

I say, *do you promise?*

He says, *yes I promise I promise,* and he has my hand in his.

He is guiding me into the wherry. He is handing me an oar. He is charging into the lake, both hands on the wood, and leaping in and pushing off. Sitting down and hunching over his oars and digging in hard.

He says, *Mar, you'll have to steer us—you'll have to guide us there. Can you do it?*

I think I cannot. I think we will never make it, wherever we are going. The surf is too high and the wind is too strong and there is lightning all around us. We are doomed; we are done. We will die out here on the lake.

But I am already dead.

I say to him, to the boy I loved and hate and love still, to the boy who has destroyed me and is saving me now:

Yes.

He says, *It won't be long now. Be brave.*

And I say, *Please, please, get me away from here.*

And he says, *I will, we will—we'll fix this—*

The waves wash so hard against us that we are nearly swamped. Out ahead, the lake is hell and hope.

He says, *Take us to Shady Bluff.*

THE SPLINTERING

I LEAVE ROSE IN Neverland. I leave the empty spaces where Nisreen and Flor should be.

I plunge into the dead-still night. I am on the lakeshore path; I am on the road and cloaked in dark, and tonight there are no stars.

Out on the lake there is a girl in a boat with one oar tight in her hands. She is staring into the rolling black and she cannot see what is ahead of her. She sees only the dark and the waves; she sees only a boy she should not trust—does not trust—but they are here together in the storm. The waves crash against the boat and foam around her feet. They will be swamped. They are out over the deepest place in the lake, where far down in the dark the names of Marshall dead poke out like stakes and wait for blood.

Out on the lake there is a girl in a boat with a boy and they are rowing for the east shore. Here on that shore I am running through the dark.

Something has broken tonight, I think. It is there, out in last summer's storm, but here inside me too. It is poison and truth and it is coming back to me in the darkness.

I am running from the men who would lock me away. I am running to the holy place where we are still honeyed gold girls.

I am running, I am running away—

THE SAFE-HAVEN

SHADY BLUFF IS EXACTLY as we left it when last summer first broke free.

I am afraid.

I should not be afraid. I should be what I am out there on the water, coming here—holding the rudder steady against the storm; steering us around the bend and into the cove; guiding us between the piers. Instead I am safe inside this house and outside the crickets chirp and chirp and there is no storm at all. Bright blankets hang over the kitchen chairs where we flung them up to dry.

It is very dark. And it is here still: that shapeless dread that met me on the sunporch and pulled me back to our second-class summer.

I should not have come here.

I say it to him:

We should not have come here.

But he is not here; I am not here. We are out in the storm and the wherry butts hard against the boat ramp, and there is a splintering of wood and the hull gives way. We are clambering out into the waves.

There is a buzzing; the buzz of lakeflies in my skull.

My belly curls into itself. On the shore I am climbing

out of the wherry and falling to my knees and that boy has my hand in his. He helps me up; he says, *It's almost over now, Margaret. Just get to the stairs.*

And I am running through the living room, through the venomed black of the air and out to the sunporch to scream down at her:

no no, do not come in here!

I do not know why I know but I know this is the moment that has ended her. Not that evening she went with a boy along the lakeshore path. Not that day he ripped her heart out on the road; not the night he did what she did not want and left her there; not the afternoon their parents said what would become of her.

All that broke apart last summer broke apart here in the storm.

I am running into the dark.

The shutters are sealed against the summer and she cannot see me smash my fists against glass that will not break. She cannot hear me scream. I am in the damp dry dark and I cannot see and there is something terrible here and something I should know. But he has my hand in his and we are running for the door and there is so much hope in me it could lift me off the ground and fly me up into the storm

and I do not know where he thinks we will go

and I do not know how we will fix this

but I will make my choice

and they will not make me leave

and I will stay here in this perfect holy place

and I am the girl who fell down into the watercolor

and he is the boy who said, *God, Mar, how did I ever get lucky enough to be born in the same world as you?*

I am digging up the key.

I am unlocking the door.

I am coming into the warmth and the light. He has my hand in his.

Outside the storm is howling and I think—far off, there is a sound like a girl shrieking, and I think the voice is my own

and she will not listen and she cannot see me before her, and it is all buzzing and buzzing and buzzing and I should not have come here

and the boy says, *Margaret—you're shaking,* and he has wrapped me in a towel and led me out onto the porch.

He has found a pack of matches and he is lighting candles, and setting an old lantern on the floor, and the glass is awash in light and everything is orange and bright and glowing.

We will come through this. We will cut this monster out.

Outside the storm is powerless and all the wind and waves in the world cannot break into our nest among the trees. Our wherry is smashed to nothing but it does not matter, and I am drenched and shivering but it does not matter, and we will find our way.

He says, *here, sit down—I'll be right back—I'll get you a blanket, I'll get you something to drink.*

I think: he is mine. He is real. He is not who he tried to be in that room with his father, or on the lakeshore, or on the road.

I think: we will come through this.

I say, *wait.*

He turns.

I am curled in the corner. There is a wicked creature in my belly but it will not consume me. They have taken my choice but I will take it back. I am here in this perfect holy lakehouse and he has come for me.

He says, *what is it?*

The wind shrieks in the trees, shrieks shrill and wild and mad and like a girl and like some feral thing.

I say:

And when at Night - Our good Day done -
I guard My Master's Head -
'Tis better than the Eider Duck's
Deep Pillow - to have shared -

He comes back to me.

He kisses me.

All around us the lantern glows and the candle-flames dance and gleam like fireflies
and they are circling and blinking and fluttering their paper wings
and we will come through this, we will
and the wind shrieks and shrieks and shrieks
and I smile into the glow
and it will be over soon
and I will be myself again
and I will be my own—

THE GRAVE

SHE WILL NOT COME to me. She is close enough to touch, aglow in lantern light and wrapped in his jacket, and no matter how loud I scream she cannot hear.

When I grab for her arm there is nothing.

I know she is not here. I know there is no lantern. I know but still I see her; still I feel the wickedness in this place. I do not know what to do or why the buzzing comes and comes or why there is music now: that song we sang late into the night with our breath frosting the air, when we danced in streetlamp light with our eyes full of stars. That old mournful song that wove August into June:

Summertime, and the living is easy—

There is music, and there is buzzing, and she is closing her eyes and curling into herself, and she is dreaming even with that creature cutting its teeth on her ribs.

She is here.

I am dizzy. I am falling in the dark, crouching here in my corner of the sunporch where the past grabbed at my throat. There is a flicker of light, like last summer bleeding back; like lantern-light and candlelight. And it is fireflies, too: one and then another and a dozen, finding me here in the dark and hovering above my hands.

There is that music, crackling with age:

So hush little baby, don't you cry—

She is here with a truth so terrible she would not believe it, but I am a different girl than I was last summer. I am a girl who did not try to kill that boy, even though I did not know why.

My hands press to the floor; to the boards that shine with firefly-glow.

There is a truth that is wrenching free, bleeding through the moth-holes in my memory; bleeding through this strange dreamt summer; bleeding up through the floor.

And the music is warped and old:

One of these mornings, you're gonna rise up singing—

I beg her to leave.

I beg her even though there is only dark; only a dead lost place where no soul would ever sit.

She will not go.

Beneath my hands the floor writhes with a thousand dying things. Lakeflies and spiders; mayflies; fireflies crushed and dead but glowing orange. And the boards are strange and gnarling and the nails poke out crooked and bent, the way my father would never allow. Planks nudge up against my palms where they should lie flat.

The music is crackling and fading and beginning again.

Summertime

She will not leave.

and the living is easy

The floor is scarred and broken. I pry the planks up, here in the corner. All the world is dead and still. The fireflies glow and I see:

I see down into the dark.

A pair of saddle-shoes, scuffed on one toe.

I fall to my knees on snagging nails and the hush of wings, of dead things and things never meant to live.

The floor is scarred and broken. I pry the planks up and I bring one hand to my mouth and clutch tight. And I see:

A pair of saddle-shoes, scuffed on one toe.

Dust and bones.

Fabric eaten away.

The walls begin to spin and spin, and the hum of wings is so loud my ears will burst, and I am bound with vines and bound to him in the water beneath the Island, and we are sinking down and down.

And I scream.

I scream for Flor, for Nisreen, for Rose. But they have been stolen away and Shady Bluff groans and creaks and last summer's waves crash on the shore.

The floor is scarred and broken. I pry the planks up and I see:

A pair of saddle-shoes, scuffed on one toe.

Dust and bones.

A gold nametag over her heart and it glows, it glows, it glows in the dead of the storm.

Her name is Margaret Moore.

THE SAVIOR

HE SAID; HE SAYS, this second-class summer: *Mar. We'll fix it.*

The lights have flickered out and died but still our candles burn. Our lantern on the floor glows off the shining planks. We sit on the sunporch together, in the south corner, where the window to the trees meets the window to the beach before it drops into the water.

I say, *I can't do it. I can't go away and give up my whole life and—*

He says, *I promised you I'd take care of it.*

I want to claw through my skin and rip out that piece of him that grows in me. We have come through the storm. We have risked our lives in a wherry that is dashed to wreckage. We have come all this way and still we have no plan.

He says, *I promised you. Didn't I?*

I stand up, staggering, and stare out at the lake. The water is black. The lamp in the bell-tower gleams so far away it feels like another life.

I say, *You promised something else.*

We are drinking tea he made while I sat alone on the porch. The cups are simple white. Mine is chipped on the rim where I knocked it against Flor's two summers ago, toasting to our last Dragonfly weekend.

He sits on the floor in his white. His hair is no longer than it was in June.

He says, *What do you mean, Mar?*

Tears gather in my eyes, but not for him. I am staring out across the water and wishing for last summer and next. My father and mother have left Shady Bluff abandoned, packed up for the end of summer, and only these unshuttered windows are left to prove it is not finished. They have driven through the dark. Their car idles at the gate. The director stands beside them in the rain, and he cannot explain where I have gone, and on the lawn there are shouts and flashlights and Deck Five has run for me. My girls that I love; my girls that I do not deserve.

The bells toll in the chapel. I cannot hear them but I know it is true.

My parents wait with their car, and in Chicago there is a plane with a seat for me, and in New Hampshire there is a narrow bed in a high attic room and all the walls are white. It will be very much like a ward, I think, or a prison, or that room in the infirmary where Nisreen talked with ghosts.

If we go to them it is all over, and only for me.

Tomorrow I will be on the winding roads to the country house. Settling into my attic room alone. Waiting for this creature to devour me from the inside out until I am only a shell and he will go on and finish this summer and next, and graduate, and go to Princeton, and never think of me again.

And I think, the way I did beneath his window: if I tell, if I say I will tell—

I turn to him. I say, *You promised you loved me.*

He looks away.

I say, *You promised.*

He looks like his father from that day when we sat in broad gold at The Poplars, when his father said, *a common whore*, and wrote a check.

The boy I loved says with his father's voice: *They were only words.*

I say, *You loved me. You did.*

He will not look at me.

I kneel down in the lamplight. I say, *Look at me. Look at me.*

Outside the wind whips branches against the glass. I wish with all I have that I had told them: that I had told Nisreen and Flor and Rose, because we have never kept secrets. They would save me from this, somehow. Take me to a doctor who could fix this one mistake that will write the rest of my life.

I say, *I loved you.*

He says, *No you didn't.*

I say, *You loved me.*

He looks. In the lantern-light his eyes are circled. He says, *It doesn't matter.*

I was wrong to come here tonight. I stand up fast and my foot sends the lantern clattering. My saddle-shoe is scuffed now, a dark mark on the leather, and it will not wash away like the mud will.

I say, *I'm going back to Marshall.*

He is beside me, standing too, and grabbing my hand. He says, *Don't.*

I say, *I'm telling the girls. I'm going to fix it—*

He says, *Mar. You'd ruin my goddamn life.*

I laugh and it is high and shrill. I say, *But you'd ruin mine. Your father, your family—you've tried—but if I tell, it's only fair—*

He says, *Mar,* and he has my hand in his.

I say, *no.*

He says, *Mar, you can't.*

I say, *It's my choice.*

He says, *You can't, I'm begging you.*

He is afraid and I am glad and this is power, I think: this is bravery. And it is only words.

I say, *I'll tell. I'll bring you down, the way you've tried to do to me.*

He says: *Margaret. I love you.*

I should not believe him. I do not want to believe him.

He says: *Everything I ever told you was true. But it isn't allowed to be true.*

He says: *We were never made to last.*

I am crying. I am sitting down on the floor in the corner, and outside the storm calms, and I don't know whether I am afraid or not.

I say, *I can't go away. I can't have a—a—*

He has my hand in his.

He says, *I promised you I would fix it.*

He says, *I'll be right back—*

I lean against the wall and look up into the shadows. And I look back to the floor, to the circle of light. There are a sickly few bugs flitting in it, moths and mayflies, and the mayflies are so fragile I do not know how they live even for their few hours. We studied them, when we were Butterflies. We caught them and flattened them to our scrapbooks, and Rose read from her guidebook while we waded and wandered. She said: *Mayflies live only on the clearest water, in streams and lakes.*

The thunder rolls. It is quieter than before. We are alone here in the dark, here in this perfect holy place, and the trees above stand sentry.

She said, *They are insects of the order Ephemeroptera. They have three stages of life: naiad, subimago, and imago.*

The floorboards creak beneath his feet. And I think he might call his father or mine; I think he might betray me again; I think I should run again, but where? And I cannot abandon him when he has chosen at last to stay with me.

Rose said, *Naiads, or nymphs, live in the water for several years and cannot fly.*

Out in the living room there is the scratch of a needle and bright mournful notes sing out from the old record player. It is that song, the one we sang wrong but with such joy and heat all through the winter that I think it is ours now.

Rose said, *Subimagos emerge at the final molt of the naiad. After a few days, or in some species only a few minutes, they molt again into their final form.*

There is a mayfly on the lantern-glass, so clear I can see through it. From the living room, the music drifts like smoke and comfort. He has come back, the boy I loved once, and he is holding something, and he sits down beside me.

Rose said, *Imagos are delicate, with membrane-like wings. They hover and court over clear water. They live only a few hours.*

We are ephemeral, I think.

I say, *Ephemeroptera. Born to linger in the water, and then grow wings and burst free and all in an instant, die—*

He says, *Mar. Don't talk like that.*

He shows me what he has found.

I say, *But that's poison. For the rats that come into the garage.*

He says, and he has my hand in his: *There was a girl back home, and this same thing happened to her, and she heard rat poison could—well. What you want.*

The container is old and dusty. It stays back in the cupboard with the cleaning things and the stacks of bright blankets. It is forbidden, I think. When I reach out to touch it my fingers draw back and will not.

I say, *Did it work?*

He tells me yes.

He tells me she did not have to go away; she did not have to give herself up. He tells me she is proud she did it; she said to his sister—her best friend—*it's up to me what becomes of me.*

I think: she did not let them write her story.

I say, *It will work?*

He says, *It will work.*

We sit quiet and waiting. The music swells and falls; it ends and catches and begins again.

I say, *How much do I take?*

He says, *Let me.*

He pours it into the tea. It is a strange chalky powder and it billows clouds in the cup.

I say, *And it will happen right away?*

He says, *Soon.*

I take the cup and hold it close.

I am afraid. I am staring into this cup and I am afraid. But I am holding my future in my hands.

I will not be a monster anymore. I will not be gnawed apart by some cold beast that sucks my blood. I will be a poet and a dreamer and a girl who sees the good in everyone.

I raise the cup to my lips. I will not be afraid. Not of pain or consequence; not of what they will do when they learn. Not of him, because he has come back to me.

I am a girl making a choice.

I drink to the bottom of the cup.

The mayflies flutter on the lamp and the storm has gone soft. The music sings, lulling and low:

One of these mornings, you're gonna rise up singing
Then you'll spread your wings
And you'll fly to the sky

There is a sharp deep pain within me. My hands clutch tight to his.

But 'til that morning, there's nothing can harm you

I do not know how long we have been waiting here. Time stands very still in the corner.

There is pain. In my belly; in my chest; behind my eyes.

The lantern is much too bright.

I am sick, I think

and the pain is blooming and blooming now

and I am curled into myself on the floor

and the colors change, and everything stains red

and everything is white and hot and pain that shoots out to the end of each finger and burns out each thread of strength in me, and I am sweating and there is something in my mouth that does not belong

and I think: *be brave.*

There is a buzzing in the air. I hear my blood in my veins and my heartbeats, loud and lurching. I am sick and I am brave, I am brave, and I say it to myself: *I am brave I am brave I am brave,* because this night will end and tomorrow is the Victory Race. Tomorrow we will be girls.

The music is too fast and too slow. It stops and begins again and my body is ripping apart, and the music sings:

Summertime—

I am curled on the floor and there is blood in my mouth and my eyes; in my throat; between my legs. The pain is so strong I cannot think

and I cannot hear the way I should

and I cannot see the way I should

and the mayflies flutter in the orange
and I want my mother and my father
and I want Rose and Flor and Nisreen
and I want to be a Butterfly asleep in a cabin on the shore
and I do not want to leave
I do not want to leave.
I do not want to leave!
All is orange and stars. All is gray and pain.
and something is wrong
and I think I am dying
and I think it has not happened by accident
and I am afraid
and I am alone
and I am all alone

THE RUIN

I LOVED A BOY once, before all this.

He killed me.

I AM MARGARET MOORE

THE UNRESTFUL

I THINK I HAVE known the truth all along.

It has been waiting beneath those moth-holes in my memory: those bruises, those gray downy spots.

I am here. I can feel the sting and tear of my skin where I pried the floorboards up. There is mud staining my socks. My Deck Five pin shines and shines.

I think I have known the truth all along:

How this summer was strange and like a dream.

How they looked too long or not at all.

How the flies swarmed thick around me.

How they whispered and whispered about Margaret Moore. Not because she was the girl who ran out into the night: because she is the girl who died.

In my last dying night I said, again and again:

I don't want to leave.

It is all I wanted: to stay and to fix what is broken. To unbury the truth.

To make my choice.

And here I am.

I have stayed.

I am already dead.

PART III

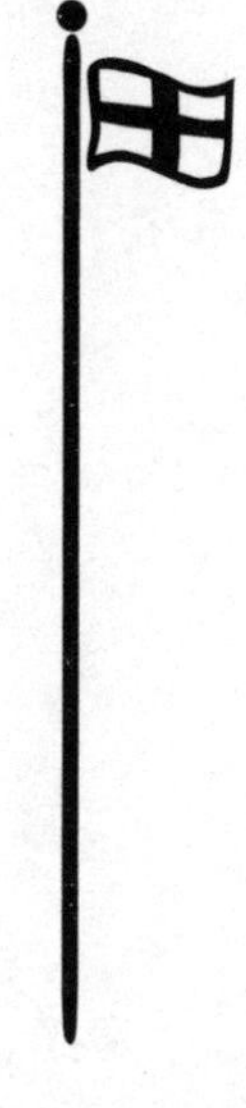

IMAGO

THE DEPARTED

I AM A DEAD ghost girl and I am walking out into the night; out of that divine place where I came and never left.

I am a dead ghost girl and I turn my back on the flat calm lake and fade into the trees. In the tunneled dark no cars pass and no lights shine through the black.

I am a dead ghost girl and I am on the lakeshore path, passing beside the cannon where it gleams and sleeps and knows. Out on the lake the *H.H. Bedford* waits untended. On the shore there is still and quiet, and the tremor of moths as they gather, and the begging beacon high atop the chapel, too far away to catch me in its light.

I am a dead ghost girl and I am coming home to Neverland, and I am climbing up the stairs, and I rest my hand on our Marshall M in the droning fanblade hum.

I am a dead ghost girl and I am home and they will find me tomorrow, my girls, and they will tell me I am wrong and real, and I will tell them what he tried to do last summer in the storm.

I am a dead ghost girl and I will live, I will tell, I will be real—

THE ABANDON

IN THE MORNING ROSE is gone.

All down the hall girls crash through doors and drip slick paths from the showers. Downstairs Deck Six rings reveille late. I am the only one who stands rooted before the room where Rose and Flor should be.

It is stripped bare. The wardrobes both hang empty; there are no tight-cornered sheets tucked to the beds. No flags cling to the walls.

The window is sealed shut now, too, and the air is

strange and stale. It is like they have been gone for weeks instead of hours: like they were never here.

I line up for roll-call.

We march to the mess.

The sun is hot enough to kill.

THE HEAT

IN THE AFTERNOON, WE run until third classmen bend and vomit. The rain-starved ground has sucked the storm away and the earth is cracking; showing its seams. The grass is brown and dead.

I am dust and bones beneath the floorboards: I saw it there before me, sharp against the summer's haze. But if I am, how does the heat still sear my skin, and how does my place in the lineup still hold, and how am I here by the lake and the trees and still my girls are nowhere?

Again, says the new counselor, and the cinderblocks come out. We run, weighted and stumbling; collapsing; staring up into a sky more green than blue. It is the color of sick and the peeling infirmary paint.

They do not speak to me and I think: has it been this way, all through our first-class summer?

I do not speak to them and I think: he has stolen my voice away from me. He has stolen my words and left me dead and stranded, and silent, and alone.

The sky behind our sycamore goes whiter; bluer; white. The leaves are not enough to soak away the sun. Sycamores are strange, dead-looking trees: dark at the roots, but as they climb the bark mottles away. High up the trunk is smooth and white.

Is it dying? Nisreen asked beneath these branches long ago, when we were Butterflies hunting Marshall trees on the list the counselor gave us. We had crossed off *catalpa*, with its great lone leaves and falling flowers. We had crossed off *tulip poplar* and *black locust.* We had wandered almost to the end of the lakeshore path, and on the lawn Deck Five drilled, with a counselor shouting, *pivot, pivot.*

I don't know, said Flor, *but the leaves match. It's a sycamore.*

Rose is always prepared, and she has her guidebook, and she finds the page and reads out loud: *The sycamore appears sick or dying, with bark that sheds partway up the trunk. This is not harmful to the tree.*

Flor says it is ugly and Nisreen says it is beautiful and Rose plucks a leaf to pin to the page. I am standing a little bit apart, and I run my fingers up the bark to where it sloughs away. Underneath the tree is smooth and cool, like bone; like what should be kept secret.

I AM MARGARET MOORE

Come on, let's go, says Flor
and they walk away off down the path
and the sun burns through the leaves and scorches the wood of our sycamore
and a girl I don't remember drops a cinderblock that thuds against the ground
and the counselor says, *again, faster, don't you dare give up*
and high up in the sky a plane is buzzing for the flyby
and they are gone: they are swallowed up into the light
and they are gone because they told; because of me
and I am alone and I am not real and it is my fault
and the sun is so bright, so bright, so bright.

THE UNDOING

NISREEN DOES NOT COME back from the infirmary.

I would go but there is no reason: our room is stripped bare, too. All that is left are those books Flor threw into my desk: *The Tragedy of Hamlet, Prince of Denmark* and *The Complete Poems of Emily Dickinson.*

I did not tell what he swore I would not.

Rose did not tell enough to hurt us. Not the things that made that boy's father lock cold eyes on me when I sat cornered before him; not the things that brought that boy into the storm.

I did not tell.

But now the words creep back and build a home within me: Rose is gone, and Flor and Nisreen too, the day after she said his name.

It is so simple she would scoff at it, I think.

THE STRANDED

I DO NOT KNOW what week it is.

I think I have slept through a day or ten. I think I have dreamt up the whole summer.

I float.

I am in the library, on the wide window-seat looking out to the water. Over my head a ceiling-fan sweeps in circles and stirs my hair. It is summer literature, hardly a class at all, and it is my favorite even though Rose and Flor say it is a waste. But it is perfect: it is, in the whirl of summer, a still place to sit and breathe. Today I linger in Greek myths beside Medusa, with her crown of fork-tongued snakes.

I am so very lonely I cannot find the words to say it.

It has been—days since I last saw Rose; since I last saw

Flor and Nisreen. They are gone and all of Marshall looks away from the space where I am not. I am the mutineer who brought a whole deck running for the storm. The thrown-away; the warning to the rest of them.

The girl who died.

I say to a Deck Four girl folded up on the sofa, *I am here.*

She looks up with her eyes unfocused.

Margaret Moore, I say. *I am Margaret Moore, from Deck Five. The girl they say is dead.*

She does not answer. The paper and the glass eat up my words so there is not even the memory of them: there is only silence.

I am not sure I spoke at all.

I go away from her. Out on the lake the sky is cloudless and the wind gusts mad and fervent. But here there is only dead still, and the pages of our books do not flutter, and the fan does not stir the air.

I come back to that Deck Four girl and she will not even look up.

I say, *I am here.*

Her shoulders hunch like she is cold; like it is winter.

I say, *Are you afraid of me?*

Her shivering gives her away.

I say, to all of them now, *Listen to me.*

They say nothing. They look away. They would make me invisible: they, and that boy, and all his family cloistered at The Poplars with sunglasses drawn like shades across their eyes.

I am so very tired that I cannot keep my thoughts in line. They spin and float unmoored, and I think, *un-Moored*, and it is right: I am without my parents and the anchor of my girls. I am without myself.

The room fades off and glimmers like I am dreaming; like I am looking up from deep down in the water, drowning and decked with weeds.

They will not look at me and I have become my silence, I think. I did not cry out for help there on the sunporch. I did not scream when that boy brought me down into the mud. I looked instead, unspeaking, to the blurring of the stars.

I have become what they have made me.

And the fear and fury gather in my lungs; gather in my mouth like lakefly wings. I am this dead ghost girl not because I am dust and bones: because I have lost my words.

I say, I shout, *I am here!*

There is nothing but the flutter of wings in my skull, and the flutter of pages beneath that Deck Four girl's hand.

I am here! I scream, and I am dizzy again I think, because the air stirs now around me: stirs with the flurry of flight.

I am here and he killed me! I shout, so loud it scores my throat, and still they cannot hear.

I am here—

and it rises deafening, silent, dead

I am Margaret Moore—

and the ghost wings sing and siege

I am the girl he killed, and you have killed me here again—

and there is a swift jagged tearing like paper and wings, and that Deck Four girl shrieks and the pages in her book rip apart

and I am running out with my saddle-shoes tapping soundless off marble. Behind me that Deck Four girl cries out again. There is a knotted murmuring and the bright sick scent of fear.

They are right to be afraid of me.

THE INTRUDER

NISREEN LIVES FAR AWAY on the other side of the world. In Jordan, where I dreamed I would go with a boy who wanted to be an explorer. There tall columns carve the canyon walls; there Nisreen rides horses fast across the heat. Her father's family has lived there for a thousand years. Her mother's family came with soldiers in dust-dulled khakis and planted scraps of England in the sand.

In the desert there are stands of palms around low pools: oases rich with water and fruit. There are mirages too, where light shimmers like water, but coming too close shatters it away.

I could never imagine it, back in our Butterfly days and piled all into Flor's bunk, telling us who we were when we were not at Marshall. I could not imagine palm trees and water so real anyone would run for them, but nothing real at all.

Now the whole world is a mirage, I think, and I understand.

It is bright out. It is wild deadly bright. I am fading down the library stairs and onto the green. Coming all apart and fluttering back together, and taking the long way around the gymnasium because I will not go into the Hall of Honor with its door that should never be opened.

I am on the Admiral's Walk looking out to the flags where that girl died in lightning.

I am in the tunnel where we stand after Parade, and it is shaded and muggy with secrets.

I am through the oak doors, slipping in when a lieutenant comes out.

I am on the stairs and they spiral up through portraits of dead men.

I am in the secretary's office and she is at her desk. Sweat slicks my forehead. She cannot see me, or she does not know she can, so I tell her, *I'm here to see the director,* but I cannot hear my words. That buzzing has come back: the buzz of shining lake-bugs and the flyby.

I think I will be sick. I think it is second-class summer again, and they have called me here to tell me I am kicked out for my secrets that could hurt a VanLandingham boy. That my parents are taking the lakeshore drive from Shady Bluff, and we will go together to that grand old Victorian and watch them dig my grave.

The secretary picks up the phone. Her lips pinch, wry. She puts it down and pushes her chair back and takes measured steps to the director's door. She goes into his office and I hear the rustling of paper; the flutter of thread-thin wings.

I am alone and when I say *hello* I hear nothing at all. The secretary comes back in with a file and leans over her desk to type out a name, and each letter comes loud and piercing, and when she looks to where I stand her eyes are empty marbles and she sees me, I think, but she will not make me real.

I am a mirage. I am Medusa and all the world is stone.

I am invisible and everywhere and I am done with waiting, and I am walking across a rug as soft as forest moss. I am stepping past the door.

The director's desk is a clutter and it is very late in the summer: late enough that he has left mugs staining rings into the wood. The cabinet drawers hang open and sweat is sleepless on the air.

I came here to speak with him: to beg him to let my girls come home to Neverland. But he is not here and anyway he would not hear me.

I am along the window, looking south and east to where that girl died; to the flags bleeding streaks into the sky. When I look back at the office they print themselves in negative, and there is something wrong about it, I think: the stars do not line up the way they should.

Something is different from when we were last here. It is too dwarfing huge to see. The more I look the more there is that buzzing in my head and in my mouth, and I think I am made of those winged bugs from the lakeshore path, and I was never a girl at all.

I am beneath the pictures on the wall, of Marshall men from last summer or last century. I am beside the cabinets with their open drawers. And I draw my thumbs across the folders inside. They are names: all of us, in real paper. My thumb is on BEDFORD, WILLIAM LAWRENCE.

Here. The answers will be here in pen and in ink, undeniable.

I peer into it. This drawer is only boys, Lower Camp boys. The top drawer of the next cabinet says on its label, UPPER CAMP GIRLS. It is half open. I grasp at it, and it strains against my fingers and I feel the blood well up, but no matter how hard I pry it will not move for my dead hands.

The secretary comes back, drifting, and I duck for the curtains before I remember. And I stand my ground instead, four steps from the drawers. She looks at me as though I am not here.

It is true: I am not.

It is less unfamiliar than it should be. I have been invisible all this dreamt summer, and all the missing winter before it, and before that too I think. I try to pin it down like wings in a specimen box: the day I turned invisible. It was not that night in the storm. That glaring gold afternoon at The Poplars instead, or that night on the shore; that blaze-hot day the nurse said *who is the boy*, when the boy said nothing at all, when I was dead in the road three feet from his car and a thousand miles from him.

The secretary pushes one drawer shut and opens another: so easy with her hands that do not bleed. She leafs through files and mumbles names: so easy for her words to bloom aloud.

She plucks a folder free and drifts out again. The Upper Camp girls' drawer hangs open.

I go to where my girls will be and the truth of what has become of them.

I look at the front for Nisreen Al-Shayab and there is only ALRIC, ELIZABETH ANNE and ALTAF, FATIMA.

There is a buzzing again, this time in my thumbs.

They have misplaced her folder.

I look back and back to find Flor but there is no Flor María Gómez de la Parra: there is GOMEZ, ANA PAULINA and then GOMEZ-AYALA, MARIA JOSE.

There is the buzz in my thumbs; the buzz in my head; the buzz inside my mouth. I am digging back to the end of the alphabet and there is a Winston, there are two Winstons. Of course there are.

They are not Rose.

They are not here.

My knees begin to give; it all begins to fade. And I grab at the cabinet and the heavy velvet curtain. I stumble back against the wall with the curtain clutched in my hand, its dust turning to dirt in my palm; the dirt turning to mud when I wipe my hand on my boat shorts. Everything is blurring gray: the space before my eyes and the space outside the window, where the screen is scratched open from a beast that wanted in or a girl who wanted out. There is no breeze.

They have thrown my girls away.

The cabinet drawer hangs open with blood on its metal track. I float my hand past where Nisreen and Flor are not. It hovers like the flies between my teeth.

I am looking for a girl named Margaret June Moore.

The names shiver before my eyes. I am in the watercolor; I am deep in the green. And the names grow wings; grow eyes; grow teeth. The air stirs up and I think the secretary has come back again, but when I look to the door she is not there and instead I see them: Nisreen and Flor together still, and Rose beside them, and they wear their Dress A's and Rose says to the director, *But you can't say Jack VanLandingham didn't have anything to do with it, you can't say it was only an accident how she died out in the storm—*

and the director is there before them, and Rose's father, and the director says, *Do you want Deck Five sent home again? Is that what you want?*

and she says, *No, sir, but—*

and her father says, *Mary Rose, she drowned out on the lake. I saw the broken wherry myself.*

and Flor says, *She wouldn't take a wherry out alone.*

and Rose's father says, *No one could've survived a wreck in a storm like that.*

and Flor says, faster now, *Well, then she was on her way to meet him, or she was running from him. Or he sent her out alone, and he knew—*

and the director says, *Would you like to be sent home, Miss Gómez, and your father to know you're slandering a good boy's name?*

and I am with them: I am close enough to grab at Nisreen's hand, to feel the brush of Flor's skirt against my leg, to feel Rose breathe out betrayal

and Nisreen says, *The truth will come out someday.*

and the director says, *Let it. But if you tell these lies again, there will be no Deck Five at all.*

and I reach for my girls and they shatter away and are gone.

I am here with the silence and the files.

There is MONTPELIER, DEBORAH ANN.

There is MOOSLEY, CYNTHIA CATHERINE.

My thumb is in the space between them and there is blood there on the page and I am nothing, and it is what I should have known, but still I stumble back.

and when I do I see the door and the portraits all around it, and he is there with a smile on his proud tanned face, he is there without care or consequence: the man from that grand old Victorian on the west shore

and the lakeflies burst in through the screen and land in my hair and my eyes

and I think I am dreaming

and I think I have lost myself

and I think it is what they wanted all along

and they are here again for one gasping breath: Rose and Flor and Nisreen, a blur before me and barefoot and drenched in rain, and it is second-class summer and it is dawn and I am drowned out in the storm and they say, *There is more there is more there is more!*

and I am stumbling out, and down the stairs, and into the tunnel, and onto the Admiral's Walk beneath the flag with its strange crowding stars, and all above me the flies buzz and buzz and the sky is dim and so very hot—

THE PRISONER

THE INFIRMARY IS THE prison too, I think.

The walls sweat. The mirrors bleed. The windows take no breeze.

I am not sure how I got to this room. I remember the sun and the buzz of the flies. I remember the even tread of marching steps against the Admiral's Walk, and how I thought *this is not safe, out here where anyone could find me,* and then—nothing.

It is evening. The light is speckled like sycamore bark; like the rust-spots on the mirror. There is dried blood souring on my thumb and trailing to my wrist. The door is missing.

I am in the haunted room. The stories are true, I think: the stories I hear even now, in whispers. From the hall there is a murmuring of Dragonflies, one room to another: *It isn't my room. It's the one on the end. A boy died there, a long time ago—*

The second Dragonfly says, *Not that boy. A girl, the one who drowned herself from heartbreak.*

I say, *No: that is wrong.*

They cannot hear me. Of course they cannot hear me.

The Deck Five girl? the first Dragonfly asks.

The second says, *Yes, a long long time ago. She died out in the storm, and the next summer she drowned the boy who broke her heart.*

There is a breeze through the window and the snap of code-flags on the firing sky. If I half-close my eyes Nisreen curls on the cot, that Butterfly summer and our first-class summer both the same.

The first Dragonfly says, *I don't think it's true. It's a story they tell us so we won't kiss boys or go out on the lake alone.*

I say, *I am real.*

The breeze goes dead. Outside it is sunset and calm; outside it is midnight and storming and *long long ago*, and my parents are cutting through low-bent trees: coming for the daughter they would send off to rot and die. Coming back to make a choice for me, with the man from that grand old Victorian and the nurse and the director and that boy and everyone, everyone but me.

I say, *Listen to me.*

In the hall there is that buzzing again: electric and pinned to the ceiling. The light is too bright for what it should be, and cold and white, and pooling on the tile.

Nisreen shifts and sighs. Flor is crouched beside her and Rose paces by the window, and it is first-class summer and Rose says, *Well, we KNOW he had something to do with it.*

Flor says, *We know he was the boy, but we don't know if he killed her or he sent her out to die or if he was there that night at all. And we can't go cursing Deck Five forever until we know the whole truth. You can't just stomp around and make your father fix it—*

And Rose says, *I know, I KNOW*, and she is digging into her curls again as though she will rip them out.

Nisreen says, beside me, *Mar. Tell us what he did.*

And I could cry or shriek or scream, and I am on my feet and they are gone and the first Dragonfly says, *She was never a real girl at all.*

I say: *I am real. I am real—*

And I am dizzy and falling and the lights hiss and snap. There is a bright flower of sparks and smoke and there on the floor is a moth, dead and huge: a singe-winged Icarus twitching still, and the cold ceiling-lights have gone dark, and the buzzing has died at last.

The Dragonflies wail. The first trips fast across the hall, and they tremble in the dark with smoke coiling up around them.

The second says, when they can breathe again: *She is real.*

They are silent now, for me.

The light fades and the fireflies come out.

THE HOME

TONIGHT I DO NOT run fearless across the lawn.

Tonight I live in the shadows. I am a wraith on the infirmary stairs; I do not wake even the Dragonflies.

Tonight there is a cover of clouds, and no moon and no stars, and I am running to Neverland. There they have not forgotten me. They still hold my place in the lineup and my seat in the mess.

I say it to myself here on the lakeshore path: *In Neverland I am real.*

The night is still and sleeping. The lakeflies gather, and the moths, and their wings haze the lights and the dark grows thick around me.

I say it to myself: *I am not this dead ghost. I am dreaming.*

The winged things swarm and swarm. Ahead of me there is the welcome gray of Neverland and I pass beneath our sycamore. They are here beyond the windows: my Deck Five girls.

I walk the old path to the door. The orange paint has dulled away. And I crouch here, one knee scabbing at the sidewalk, and it is not that old cracked path where we line up for roll-call every summer. It is new and whole.

I say it to myself: *They cannot erase us. They will not.*

But our bright rebellious paint is gone.

I stand up. I tread the new wrong sidewalk and now I am here. Now I am before the doors to Neverland.

They are shut.

I grasp at the knob and it will not turn. I am a dead ghost girl and they have locked me out of Neverland. They have locked my girls away from me.

There is nothing, there is nothing I can do. Above me the light in the eaves looks down and there is that lake-swarm gathering, and it is a still unbroken night and I am all alone. And I bring my dead hands back and hit the door—the little window in the door. I hit with all my strength.

I hit the window. I hit and hit and there is blood on my hands and I do not know if it is real. I am cracking my palm against the glass now, against the blotted red, and the sting burns through and it is all I want in all the world: to press my hand against our Marshall M.

I scream into the dark: *Deck Five! I am here!*

The blood trails down my arms and I am on my knees, I think, and the lakeflies tangle their feet in my hair; the moth-wings graze my skin.

Above me the glass gleams clean. There is no blood at all.

And now it is darker still and now it is blinding bright and we are spinning in the diamond drops and we are nine years old; we are fifteen; we are girls. And the fireflies glow bitter on my tongue so I cannot make the words but only think in the dark and the pale:

Flor. Nisreen. Rose.

I can feel them here the way I could in the infirmary: beyond the walls, together, and Nisreen says, *She is gone again.* It is second-class summer and we are here, we girls, but I am out on the lawn throwing rocks at his window. I am out on the green with him leading me away. I am on my back beneath the cannon and the stars.

Rose says, *We have to do something. We have to DO something, and I don't know what, and I don't know why she's shut us out—I don't know why she won't tell—*

It is a pain like the pain when I died on the floor: I have torn us apart.

Flor says, *It isn't always as simple as you want it to be.*

And Rose says, and it is hot with rage and loss: *We're Deck Five. Bound with our sisters 'til the grave, and doesn't that mean anything—why doesn't she know we would kill for her, die for her—*

All around me is the stink of mud and gunpowder, and the cold stare of stars far-off, and I am here and there and nowhere at all. In my place is something that hungers beneath the floorboards. Something with black eyes and gray wings; something downy and mindless, with veins that tether it to that deep place in the lake.

I can feel its pulse; the pulse it has robbed from me. I can hear its wet cellophane wings.

I do not believe in monsters.

No: that is wrong.

I do not believe in monsters that curl beneath girls' beds and suck their blood.

I believe in monsters with wide smiles, beautiful and bright, that live in grand old Victorians; that push girls into the mud; that take our voices and tell us what we are.

The breeze breathes through the sycamores. The monster hums low and content.

I have come too late to this place, I think.

The moths brush their wings against my eyes. The monster drinks me all away and they say, in whispers, *There was once a girl who drowned herself from heartbreak. She died out in the storm, and the next summer she drowned the boy who broke her heart* and it is dark and brilliant

and we are in the watercolor

and we are in the green green blue
and my arms twine around his neck
and I am pulling him down
and he is my love and I am his
and he will sail the world single-handed and I will write poems that sing and sing
and the green weeds float away from his face and he is not a boy he is a monster with downy wings bent in the water and black eyes and a mouth too wide
and I did not try to kill us
and I did not try to drown him
but I would, I would, I would—

THE RESTING-PLACE

THE *H.H. BEDFORD* IS moored out where the shallows sink into the deep.

I stand on the shore of Lake Nanweshmot with my hand on the cannon; with my blood soaking into it. My saddle-shoes suck into the mud. If I look down I will see a girl there at my feet, but I do not look down. I look out at the tar-black lake and the ghost ship at her mooring.

I am all alone tonight.

I step into the lake. There is a cannon at my back and my feet stir the water to gray, and there are vines around my ankles and wings in the dark. I could sink into the mud or drift away into the sky: I could let the water take me in.

I could die, I think, the way he meant me to. Instead I am walking out and out.

The water is up to my waist now. I am not afraid.

If I look back I will see far down the shore; through the trees; around the point. I will see the gray of Neverland at the edge of the wild.

I do not look back.

The water is up to my neck now. I am not afraid. I let my saddle-shoes peel away from the mud and I am pulling through the water, as silent as sin.

Ahead of me the ship looms. Her sides are white-painted wood. From close along her she is not the smooth stretch she seems to be from the shore: she is rough planks nailed together. She is spun with spiderwebs; she is spotted with scampering legs.

There are no holds to climb her but there are round life-preservers hung along the stern to dry. I am clawing at her hull. She will not bow down to help me. And those bright circles hanging down are so high above my head and I am so very tired, and I think: I could sleep here, in the water. I could float.

I could drown here in the lake.

But I am not a girl who drowns herself from heartbreak.

I claw at the hull. I strain with grasping hands. At last the stars light up for one stunned moment and the rope is mine.

I cling with all my life. The rope in my hand is a warm welcome pain and I am real. I can see the shore: the lakeshore path, and the circles of lamplight, and two lieutenants walking brisk beneath them. They do not look out to the water. They do not even think of the ship, because she is only a ghost ship: she is only a trapped thing who cannot free herself.

I am weak from the monster that sucked my strength away and the poison that boy fed me. But I am here and climbing higher, and at last my hands find the rail and my foot swings up and hooks into the ring.

I fall to the deck.

My foot is tangled in the ropes. Blood trickles down my hand. I am on my back and I am looking up into the sky. There are no stars tonight but there were stars that night last summer, here on this deck with a boy. These bare masts know our secrets.

Tonight I tell them another:

I loved a boy once, before all this.

I say to the masts; to the boy who is beside me:

I will find you here, before summer is over. We will stand close the way we did beneath the sun when you were afraid—when you saw me dead with mayflies where my eyes should be and lips that spill deep red.

We will stand close enough for dancing: held fast with nails that closed my grave.

You will take me in your arms again and I will ask you why.

I will say: tell me you are sorry.

I will say: make it right. Bring my girls back home to me, and my father and mother too, and lead them to that place where you watched me die, and tell them what you did, and tell them it was wrong, and tell them you loved me then and you love me still.

You will choose.

And if you are the boy you were those months we were in love, I will forgive you.

And if you are not, you will see the truth: that I am a poet and a dreamer and a girl who sees the good in everyone, and I am a monster too.

I am cold and bleeding.

I am warm and glowing and with him.

I am all on my own and the ghost ship hangs weightless over mud and vines and ruin.

I sleep safe on my trapped ship.

HANNAH CAPIN

THE GOLD

I WAKE TO CANNON-FIRE.

I am on my back and staring at a sky the color of nothing. My skin is tight with dried-out lakewater; with mud. My shirt is stained. The skin on my hands is ripped away where I clawed up from the depths.

I stand up and come to the port side. All is still. There is mist rising and the water is a delicate purple-gray, and I think: soon summer will end.

On the shore the boys who fired the cannon are marching away. Across the dew and the faded green, the color-guard raises the flags. The reveille bells ring. And then, above them, there is the deep tolling of the lowest bell in the carillon. Tolling and tolling, patient and even, and marking today apart from all the blurring summer days.

Today is the Gold Star Ceremony.

Across the road it is our very first Marshall summer and I am slinging my sash across my shoulder. My face is red with sunburn and my knees are pink with poison ivy and I have never looked so perfect in my life. I have not held our banner yet, like Rose. I have not called the step, like Flor. I have not won the horsemanship award like Nisreen, who rides better than the first-class girls even though we are only Butterflies. I have gazed too much into the leaves and the stars. I have won my badges, but I have not won honors: not until today, on this last Saturday of summer. Today I will lead the processional march up the aisle of the chapel.

The sun warms.

We line up for roll-call and march to the mess.

When the bell tolls again I am lying in the lifted space behind the great round wheel. Above me is the mizzen-mast and I am finding all the secrets in the sails. I rise up into sun so bright it turns to gray. Ahead of me the Admiral's Walk spills over with Butterflies and first-classmen; with Naval One and Deck Five, and all in our Dress A's. It is beautiful sharp chaos, a dozen different steps called; feet marching in fierce time up to the chapel and into the dark.

Today we honor the Marshall dead. We honor the ones who died in trenches; who died at sea; who died in firefights high above the clouds. Today I am a ghost at the helm of my ship and I think: there was once a girl who died alone on the floor of Shady Bluff.

High up the bell still tolls. The boy who killed me waits in the chapel, washed in promise.

I leave the helm untended and come up to the bow. All is bright and burning, and I say in the gray to the boy I did not kill: *I am here* and I am climbing up and letting go

and I am slipping into the water and the waves stir up and take me in

and I am gliding through the clear; skimming over it like a mayfly; I am dead and I am immortal; I am Ephemeroptera.

I am on the shore. I am coming up into the mud where the cannon stands guard.

I am running now, across the green in the heat of the sun, and ahead Deck Six files in two by two with a lieutenant at each door.

I am at the crest of the hill and I fall in with them. The high doors swing shut behind us. The tolling quits. Lakewater pools invisible around my saddle-shoes.

We find our seats in silence; we crowd the wooden pews. The aisle is long and the air is striped light and dark.

The drummer boys begin their march. The procession moves forward all together, to the slow solemn cadence, and the Butterfly at the front holds her flag high, and my arms begin to ache.

I stand alone with weeds in my hair and mayflies fluttering close. The procession halts. And I am shimmering in and out again, and time is still and spinning. Now an Aviation boy reads names and now a Deck Two girl, and they glide up to the rafters. The ghosts gather in droves.

I am here for the boy who made me one of them.

The Deck Two girl says, *Norman Haskins. Paul Hawthorne.* High up in the balcony six first classmen stand at attention, and after each dozen names they shout: *They fought with courage and died as Marshall men.* I am not thinking of the boys who died at Château-Thierry; at Pearl Harbor. I am thinking of the dead whose names will not be read.

They say, *There was once a girl who drowned herself from heartbreak. She died out in the storm, and the next summer she drowned the boy who broke her heart.* They are wrong: he will never die. He will live forever in the Hall of Honor and on plaques atop new buildings; in sons who march with Naval One; in handshakes and behind closed doors; in cars that speed and shine.

I am dead beneath the floorboards.

Up high those six first classmen shout, *They fought with courage and died as Marshall men.* Behind them there is the board; there are mothers and sons of the Marshall dead; there are Winstons and Bedfords and VanLandinghams. It is where Rose and Flor would stand if they had not been sent away. It is where he stands: I am sure of it.

I look up.

In the balcony there are only strangers.

He is not where he should be: he has hidden himself from me. He is a coward now.

I turn away and search the rows of shoulder-boards and

neat-trimmed hair. The names ring and hum and it begins again: the flickering that has scarred my sight since the night I robbed my grave. It is a veil that falls away, and what is real is gone and instead there is light and shade that tempts me in. The air turns hot and close.

I look up.

He is there—he is here—he is with me again, high-up the way he was when I begged beneath his window. He stands with his eyes ahead and his family behind him.

I say, and it slips watery through the melting light: *Tell me you are sorry.*

He does not look down to where I stand.

I say: *Tell me you will make it right.*

They shout and I hear his voice in it: *They fought with courage and died as Marshall men.* But the veil is falling down again and he is gone and I am alone beneath him with my blue-dead skin that damns us both.

I say: *Tell, or I will tell—*

And I am running now, to the back of the chapel. I am climbing the stairs. He is gone, or I am, and I cannot tell the difference: I cannot tell anymore what is real. But still I am gasping his name at the back of the balcony. He is gone and I am caught behind an iron wall of three great Marshall families.

And then.

And then.

I see who is in front of me. A Winston, a *damn* Winston: even kicked out she could never be gone from here. She has come back for this with her father in his careless smile and her grandfather in his uniform. With all her Winston cousins.

There is a bloom of blond-brown curls. There is a jut of shoulders I would know anywhere.

I say, *Rose!*

She turns.

She can see me, I know it, and I say it all in a rush—

It was Jack VanLandingham in the wherry, and he fed me poison and watched me die, and he lied and lied, and tell—and take my blood and stain his name—

The Bedford man beside her slips his arm around her shoulders, and down below they read another name, and the Winston woman blinks and breaks us.

She is not Rose at all. She is some aunt: my mother's age instead of mine. When she reaches up to take that man's hand there is the glisten of gold on her finger.

She is real and real and staring, still, into my eyes, and she is not Rose, and still I swear on our gold M: she is.

I say *I will tell*

and the names ring out and out: all the names but mine.

They have gone away and left me in the burning cold. And all that is left is that space beyond the veil where I can see what should have been. There is rot in my heart, and hope that taunts and swells the floorboards shut.

I say, because this time I remember how: *no.*

And I am flying out away from the woman who is not Rose. I am flying up in a spun-tight spiral into heat and light, and up the stairs to the carillon room, and up and up to the room above: the hell-hot room with the bells.

It is second-class summer and we lie splayed across the floor with my head against his heart; with the salt of his lips on mine.

We are bright and in love. We were not a mistake.

and I say: *He killed me*

I say: *He killed me*

I say: *I am here I am here I am here*

and the dark closes in but up high in the eaves there is humming and wings, and the bells nudge awake

and a white flash of light

and the bright ripping pain from that night on the floor

and a sound so exultant I think it will kill me

and it is the bells and they clang high above

and they sing and they shout and they wake the whole world.

I am under the floorboards and loud in the sky.

I am in the dead dusk with my love and I say

I will tell I will tell I will tell—

I will kill you the way you killed me—

THE STORY

THEY SAY: *THERE WAS once a girl who drowned herself from heartbreak.*

It is a whisper in the dark of the carillon room. It is a murmur one Dragonfly to the next on the woodland path the last Saturday of summer, and we will float in the water and watch the decks sweat and shout at the oars and on the bucket brigade. It is a promise on the lips of the Deck Five girls. They ache with loss but still they sing with scarred unbroken pride: still they leave her place in the lineup.

They say: *it was summers and summers ago, forever ago I think.*

It is only a story and I am a ghost: a ghost with flowers blooming through my bones and butterflies that crowd to sip my blood.

I whisper through the veil: *You are not the boy you were those months we were in love.*

It wends across the lake and carves deep ripples where there is no breeze. The leaves sift and sigh, and the flags breathe on their masts, and the Dragonflies snatch at tendrils slipping from their braids and tuck them behind their ears. And now they are walking faster; now they have left the path; now they run like deer across the drill-field; now my promise seeps into the grass and fills the hollow place with truth.

They say, and I say with them: *She died out in the storm, and the next summer she drowned the boy who broke her heart—*

I am a girl. I am a monster too.

THE REGIMENT

IT IS THE LAST Saturday of summer. The bells have rung out from the chapel and we have run and sailed and rowed. Evening has crept across the grass and we say: *tonight we join the Regiment.*

Tonight we will sail our First-Class Sail aboard the *H.H. Bedford.* Tonight we will drop our names down into the waiting water.

We are almost out of time.

We Deck Five girls crowd all into one bathroom. We are in Dress A's, not school-dance dresses. Our hair is in braids. And still we fuss: we straighten our ribbon-racks and our shoulder-boards and our nametags, stuck fast to our blouses.

I AM MARGARET MOORE

In the mirror I am a real girl, as real as any girl has been. But when I open my mouth to speak my blood begins to spill.

Long ago, beneath the trees at Shady Bluff, my father told me stories of his Marshall days in winter school. Of hunts on horseback through the woods, and cold smoke air, and rifle-shots. Of the first kill: how the fox would heave its dying breath, and an older boy would wet his hand and paint in red across the younger boy who brought his first beast down. In photograph, he stood proud and new and fourteen, with stripes below his eyes. *The blooding,* he said, and I cried for a fox that died a dozen years before I was born.

In the mirror I am a real girl. I touch my fingers to my lips; I sweep them along my cheeks. I say to myself, to the hunter and the prey: *Tonight I will see through the veil. Tonight I will keep my promise.*

When we are perfect we walk out all in a row. The other girls hang off the railings with their arms absentminded around each other and their eyes flickering back our glow. It is the first time we will march without them. Just us first-class girls in matching columns, marching the lakeshore path with gold-orange light pouring down our backs.

In the savage sunset light their cheeks match mine. My blood has marked us all.

The boys stand at parade rest: the naval companies first, and then Band and Troop and Aviation. On our side, Deck One is at the front and Deck Six is last, behind us.

The reg com calls, *First Class, attention.*

The reg com calls, *First Class, present arms.*

All down the path our arms snap into place.

We say, *Sir, the First Class requesting permission to come aboard, sir.*

It is thunderous.

The reg com says, *You have permission.*

We march out. At the end of the pier, the *H.H. Bedford* waits. She is a ship we know like our own names: the rough of the planks and the strain of the ropes as we soar up and up in the rigging and let the sails fly. She is a swift magnificent thing caught in this lake. She will lie at her moorings all summer, and each winter they will beach her, flightless, with frost on her hull.

I want with all my heart to set her free.

We come aboard in the molten light of sunset. The water is flat and gold. We crowd on, girls to starboard, stringing our elbows together like the paper-doll chains we cut in our Butterfly cabins. I am arm-in-arm with a girl I have never met; *Beatriz Asturias,* her nametag says. Past her is a Winston cousin with the same blond-brown curls as Rose.

The motor thrums to life. A great cheer rises up, and on the pier two ensigns wave us off. Tonight there is no crew in the rigging. The captain stands at the wheel and a half-dozen ensigns wander the deck, but this night is ours.

We circle the lake in the dying sunset. Marshall spreads before our starboard side, with three girls running in miniature across the drill-field, and down at the end of the lake-shore path there is Neverland. Deck Five shouts and shouts and waves semaphores. They are a galaxy of girls, so close to the woods that the trees could swallow them up.

From out here they are not Marshall girls at all. They are something all their own.

The Winston cousin says, *Remember, back in Butterflies, the summer it always rained—*

We are sailing past town; past the grand old Victorian with its wide porch.

The girl beside me says, *Remember—Jessica, remember when you saw a ghost in the bell-tower,* and Jessica says, *there's no ghost! It was only birds*, and the Winston cousin says, *if there's no ghost, who rang all the bells that summer—*

We are sailing past the point of land where that girl with the parlor-smile lives in the summer, and out on the lawn they are playing croquet, all of them in white. Music drifts over the water, blurred, like a painting left out in the rain.

I unlink my arms from theirs. I slip between them to the main mast: the mast that was mine long ago. Tonight her sails are bound tight as I climb into the sky. It is coming home, to reach the top of this highest mast, where the wind blows fresh and the world is spread before me. I step onto the footrope with my arms around the foreroyal yard; with my red-stained fingers digging at the canvas.

There is wind in my hair and blood on my face. I am close enough to touch the veil: to reach through it and make him mine the same as I am his. I do not know which of us is real. But I am finding the place where he should stand, one hand on the bowsprit and the other shading his eyes.

I fix my sight on the stranger in his place.

I say: *I am yours. You are mine.*

I will break the veil tonight.

We are sailing on toward the wild of the south shore. It is not wild anymore, and maybe it never was. Maybe only our little-girl selves saw it that way, when we would sail close to the bank and peer up at the bungalows dotting the cliff. They are gone now, all of them, and new homes have sprung up in the quiet of winter. They hang so huge they could press the cliff flat. Wood stairways veer down to piers and boats, and everything is newer than it seems it should be, as though Lake Nanweshmot has not yet decided they belong.

I stare and stare at the reg com's place. The wind draws water from my eyes. I begin to see it, the more I think of him: his face, his eyes the flicker-black they were the night he watched me die. Black but shining orange in lamplight, and glittering with the blinding light of after, and I say to him:

why

and the veil shimmers for an instant and comes tumbling back again.

We are sailing up the east shore now. We are curving in close and the old lakehouses swim in the embers of dusk.

And I say: *I have come back for you.*

I am near to where he killed me. I can feel us there, last summer, glowing hallowed in the dark. I say: *I have never left this place. I will keep you here with me.*

It will be here, I think. Here off the shore of Shady Bluff I will find him through the veil. It must be here.

I tip my chin back and look up at the sky. The sky, the sky: here on Lake Nanweshmot it is my favorite thing, even more than the water and the trees. No matter how many summers pass, the same sky still looks down. To the stars, peeking out through the fading light, it is a thousand years ago, and I have not stepped off that pier and fallen into the green.

I have not died. I have not even lived.

Far down below a girl says, *There it is. Up ahead, the haunted house.*

I could stare at the sky forever. I could live in this moment forever. I am, already, I think. I am as old as my grandmother, and I am sitting in the shade of the sycamores; in the sweet decay of browning white catalpa-blossoms, and I am knitting a lumpy and hideous blanket, and when my granddaughter and her friends swim out too far into the cold and come back with their skin turning blue I will wrap them in blankets they will pretend to hate, but love in secret. I will say, *This moment is endless*, and it will bind them to this night.

I will tell them how I drowned the boy who killed me.

Another girl below says, *Look at it—you can see it has a terrible secret. That's why no one has stepped foot inside, not since that summer—*

I drop away from the sky and there in front of me is the lakehouse I love. It is not grand and storied like that Victorian or new like the houses on the cliffs. It is an east shore house: a lakehouse to its bones. White wood and trees and waves lapping close.

There it is in front of us: the lakehouse I love.

It is wrong. The trees hang too low and the grass is untended and the vines, the vines grow up and up and curl around the windows. The sunporch is shuttered tight. And the paint is peeling, and the letters have faded at the glare of all summer under this great sky. The wild has come too fast to Shady Bluff: to swallow my home and my grave.

It's beautiful, says a girl who has never stood on that beach with lake in her hair. She has not sat on that sunporch when light streamed through; has not dozed in the little bedroom upstairs with the windows flung wide and the stars spilling in; has not bled her life out on the floor.

I wonder, says the girl who believes in ghosts, *what really happened.*

We are almost past it now, and the captain is guiding us around the place where the land tucks back in. In a moment we will be out over the deepest water. They are whispering again, and running their thumbs over their nametags, and murmuring wishes and prayers.

But I am staring still at Shady Bluff. The vines flourish untamed because my mother will never come back and cut them away. The paint peels because my father will never haul out the ladder and paint a fresh black coat over the letters that tell everyone, everyone who sails by, that this is Shady Bluff and it is ours.

It is forgotten. It belongs to the woods, to the lake, to its secrets.

And I see it, while everyone else looks away—

the trees bending low

and the vines climbing up

and the walls growing great long cracks from the earth to the roof.

It is shut like a coffin but it bursts open too, and the secrets spill out and no living soul can see them.

My eyes are blurring now, again, and my dead heart beats too fast. And I say to him: *See what you have done.*

I say: *See what I will do.*

and below she says—the girl who sees ghosts—*Remember—*

THE VEIL

AND SHE SAYS *REMEMBER*

and it is dark and blinding bright and the sky pours fire across the lake

and she says *Remember*

and Nisreen says, down below me, *Remember our first Marshall summer, when we watched the First-Class Sail from our Butterfly cabin, and Mar said—it would be us before we could blink—*

and she is light and mayfly wings

and arm in arm with Flor and Rose

and we are aglow on our First-Class Sail

and Rose says, *If only she could tell us—*

and Flor says, gazing hawkeyed to the shore, *Well, we blinked, and she's gone.*

and Nisreen says, *Mar.*

She is looking up at me. She is here and as real as she ever was in that narrow bed across from mine, or turning gold under the sun on the pier, or gathering shells, or swept against Flor.

She says *She is here* and it ripples out and spoils the sight of her: circles spreading over the water.

She says, *Mar. Tell us it was him, tell us what he did, tell us what to do*

but I am climbing down, falling down, and landing hard on hands and knees, and stumbling up and rushing fore

and off in the brilliant deep of the shore Shady Bluff stands unbowed again

and there is a shout from just ahead: *First Class, attention*

and I have found him.

He is beautiful and bright. He is the sun and the stars and the lightning that broke across Lake Nanweshmot that night in the storm, and he is lantern-light on the floorboards, and I have found him again at last

and I say: *There was once a girl who drowned herself from heartbreak.*

He is as he has always been: the boy I fell in love with on the shore. There is the scar on his brow; there is the little furrow that deepens when he talks about his father. There is the light in his eyes the way it was when he told me he wanted to be an explorer.

I say: *It was summers and summers ago, forever ago I think.*

He is here before me and I ring my arms around his neck. I ring my hands around his throat.

And I say, *She died out in the storm, and the next summer she drowned the boy who broke her heart.*

Here is what I mean to do:

I will crush his voice between my hands

and push him back against the bow

and hold him close, and we will fall

and the lake will rise to bring us home

and I will swim down and down until he breathes his ragged last

and the blooding streaks across my face will stain the water red

and we will die together.

I say: *She drowned the boy who broke her heart—*

I am crying. I can taste it on my lips: the salt of tears and the copper bite of blood.

My hands press tight against his skin. I rest against his chest and feel his heartbeat singing through my skull. We will sail into the sun and I will write words and forget that awful night. We will come through the storm.

I say: *She drowned him—she did—*

but it spills into the water and the light and I am dreaming. I am burning with fever and rotting beneath the floor. I am dust and bones and the end of our very last summer. Soon I will be only a stirring breeze that rings the bells and kills the boys who lure me from the shallows: soon I will be a watercolor blur of what was not and what will never be.

He is blinding proud noonday and I am dust and bones and dark
and nothing
and nothing

THE BURIAL

THE REG COM SAYS, *First Class, attention.*

I have ripped back through the veil again and fallen to the deck. My sight spins with stars and splinters sew my hands.

He is gone. In his place is a boy I have never seen before. It is wrong: it should be someone Marshall through and through, here for nine summers, who wins reg com our last week. It should not be some new stranger whose photograph will hang forever in the Hall of Honor: *Regimental Commander, Final Make.*

I could not kill the boy I loved. I love him still, I think.

The captain cuts the motor. The silence pours in and the ship glides slow and stealth across the lake. Above us the sky is fading.

The reg com says, *First Class. Tonight we join the great tradition.*

The reg com says, *Tonight we are eternal.*

He does not call the at-ease. But he pivots sharp to port side, and it ripples from the bow. We crowd tight: everyone but me has found our place. Ahead of us the shore looms, and out past our starboard side the Island floats alone, and the lights atop the Naval Building blaze.

I walk aft down the long bare stripe of deck.

The lake is dark and deep. Far down in the black there is gold, untarnished by mud and time. Far down there is a girl with her fingers laced around a boy's neck. She is swimming down and down, and through the watercolor, and into what lies beneath.

At port and starboard the first classmen unpin their names and hold out gleaming pieces of themselves. We drift suspended on the water. And from the secret depths there is a burst of life, and bubbles stream like fireworks for the surface, and they have breathed their last—the girl who died and the boy who killed her, and they are locked into each other's arms. The cold resplendent agony of drowning tears their lungs apart but not their hands.

We let go.

Our names rain down on Lake Nanweshmot. A hail of names; a storm of girls that breaks the still and dives into the dusk. We are eternal.

The captain chokes the motor to life.

The magic shatters: time moves on again. There is the

chug of the motor and mumbling from the ensigns. The lights on the shore glow brighter.

We are sliding on and leaving them behind. I think there is the faintest glitter of gold in our wake. Our names twenty feet down, and then fifty. Darting down to join that Winston uncle who died at sea with an anchor tattooed on his arm but the Marshall M over his heart. Fading to land where I tangle dead together with a boy: my hands still wound around his neck; our heartbeats matched at last.

First Class, the reg com says. *Attention.*

I could not drown him.

First Class, the reg com says. *Present arms.*

We are pulling into place along the pier. Ahead the path before the Naval Building crowds thick with decades of our regiment.

An ensign leaps off the *H.H. Bedford* and slides the gangway into place. The captain cuts the motor again and silence hushes in. It is like a dream, I think: I am here with my regiment and drowned with our names and nowhere at all.

The reg com calls the order-arms and they are coming ashore. Boys first and then girls. The bugle sounds taps. There is still that dread in my stomach like I will be sick; like it is last summer again and that piece of him grows within me.

I could not kill him with my dead hands and my heart still beating in my birdcage chest.

The blood across my face is all my own.

I stand alone on my ship as the first classmen pivot off the pier and onto the lakeshore path, before the alumni regiment. And there they are, with the Winstons on one side and the Bedfords on the other.

They are not in uniform but matching anyway, and their class rings glow against the tan of summers well lived in the ease of the porch and the sloping lawn of The Poplars; in the shine of new cars that speed down drives without a thought to who waits past the bend. It is too dark to tell them apart.

The reg com calls, *Left face.*

I am cold, so very cold I think it is the winter.

The reg com calls, *Forward march.*

The first class takes the lakeshore path. They vanish two by two into the dark. I glide up to the bow again and take his place, my hand against the bowsprit.

The regiment stands silent on the shore.

All that is left is the blood on my face and the girl on her back in the mud. And she thinks, she whispers:

Though I than He - may longer live
He longer must - than I -

It is all a dream from a girl who never was: from every girl who never was. I begin to wonder if I was ever a girl who was real. I begin to wonder if there has ever been a girl who was real: a girl who said, *This is what I am,* and made it real.

On the lakeshore there is the cannon that gleams, and beyond it there is the family whose son left me here a long summer ago, and beyond them the code-flags stand spotlit on high

and he says, and he is a world away: *First Class, you are the Regiment*

and he says, *First Class, you are eternal*

and he says, *You have always known what you are—*

THE LIES

TIME HAS BROKEN. ITS edges, fraying all summer, have snapped free.

It is night; it is day. I am parched with thirst and when the sun burns me to ash I climb down from my ship and float in the lake. The water tastes of mud and vines. I do not care. I am a wild unbound girl.

In the hot death of afternoon the drill-field teems and teems. Tomorrow is the Valor Race, if tomorrow comes when it should, and the day after is our Victory Race. All the camp buzzes with runners on the tearing sprint up the hill to the archery range; with girls shouting on the bucket brigade, hauling water from the lake and passing it hand over hand to fill a barrel; with boys churning up the wherry course. The code-flags come up and down on the Naval Building. Boats sail in wind so strong they should not dare.

Deck Five is close and off to ourselves. I am with them, breathing into the sails; scribbling code-flag letters; cheering myself hoarse. It is us against the world and against the lies.

It is only a race. It doesn't matter.

It is everything.

If I close my eyes until the white light bakes to orange I can see them beyond the veil: Rose with her notebook and Flor with her semaphores and Nisreen with her pen, writing words. It is only a thread that keeps me from them. It is only a thread that tethers me to what is real.

Real, I say, when I myself am not.

They say, the Deck Six girls who swim out to my ship on the Victory route: *Don't stop in the water. She killed him here, you know*—and then they race back for the shore with their lies like flies around them.

And I think: the story is real and I am not.

I AM MARGARET MOORE

The girl who drowned herself from heartbreak, the Deck Six girls say, rising up to stand in the mud, *for a boy who never loved her at all.*

They were not here those star-struck nights when all the world was ours. They were not here when he told me truths he told no one else. But who can say those nights were real at all, when the truth has died with me?

She killed him, they say, stretching out their arms beneath the sky, about that wherry-boy whose name I can't remember. I am here in the water, and floating and floating, and real and not.

She killed him, they say, and a shout rises up on the shore. And he is beyond the veil and past reproach, and safe behind my silence.

He is cloaked beneath my fever-dreams so I cannot find him even when he commands the regiment. He is here and not, his back to me, sailing single-handed out beyond the Island. He is skimming past my grave and he does not falter: he looks only to the line of the waves and the snap of the sails, and he swings the tiller and frees the sheet and tacks hard through the header, and tomorrow he will lead Naval One to win the Valor Race.

I hate him so much it burns through my veins and bleeds black into the water.

I hate him because he lied, but I hate him more because he did not. He told me the truth when he said he hated his father; when he said he would sail off and leave his name behind. But he threw me away and he kept his lies instead.

I hate him because he sat silent while his father called me a whore and wrote a check.

I hate him because he let our parents wrest my fate from me.

I hate him because in the end he did not hate me at all, and he killed me still.

They say on the shore, *She killed him.*

I am only dust and bones.

THE VAGABOND

NIGHT FALLS AGAIN.

I wade alone in the shallows with the mud sucking at my shoes. When the fireflies flicker I see a girl on the shore, her hands twined with a boy's, and she glows with a light that cannot last. And I blink and she is gone, and I think: *go home, Margaret, and leave him.* It is not that I do not believe in love. I do, I do, with all that is left of my heart.

It is that I do not believe in him.

Go home, Margaret, I say, and I do. I rise from the lake

with water running down my legs; with moonlight painting my bones.

I am a small beast with downy wings.

I am a wild creature with matted hair and eyes that have turned from blue to black. My skin pricks new with spines.

I am a beast with broken teeth and a knife stuck out of my chest. It has cracked my ribs and split my belly, and inside there is nothing at all: only a hollowed space where secrets bleed out.

I am a dead ghost girl, abandoned and wandering. My ribs catch on my ragged cotton shirt. I am poisoned and going mad: I have always been mad, I think. We are all mad, we poet-girls, we girls who sing and strew flowers; we girls who wear short skirts and fall into the sort of love that is not chaste and clean—the sort of love that is shouting and wild and makes us forget everything else.

We are all mad, we girls.

I am a mad girl who walks the lakeshore in mud up to my ankles. I swim in moonlight; I float above that deepest place and do not fear the things beneath. I wake when the sun comes up and the cannon fires and I am sleeping here on the water, and the mist is all around me, and everything is still, and I am Medusa and all the world is stone. I think: we should lie dead ninety-nine feet down. He should be dead, the way the stories tell it, and I should be let go at last, and I should be redeemed.

I think I will not find him through the veil again. I could not kill him even if I did.

I think that he has won.

I come ashore and climb high in the trees where the branches are too thin to hold. I wait there, in the heat of day, and far below the Butterflies come marching through. They wear boat shoes and knee socks. They are sweating girl-sweat, and their hair curls into tendrils on their necks, and they march one after the next along the path to the lake. It gleams through the trees and shouts to them.

The last girl tarries behind the rest, and her hair is the color of flax.

I am a mad girl who sleeps in a tree and does not fear the fall.

It is strange and wild here in the woods, even close enough to Marshall to hear the cannon and the toll of the bells; even close enough to see the bright flutter of the code-flags through the leaves.

It is night and day and night again.

The air hums. The lakeflies buzz around me and I do not swat them away. They crawl on my arms; on my lips and my eyes. The vines grow too fast, Virginia creeper and poison ivy, but it will not poison me. I doze and I wake and when I have opened my eyes a vine binds my legs to the branch where I sit.

I am a mad girl alone in the wild. And I whisper four

lines of poetry, and they crack my lips and draw blood. I say:

And now We roam in Sovreign Woods -
And now We hunt the Doe -
And every time I speak for Him
The Mountains straight reply -

It is sunset. The light is gold through the green.

I say, the way I did on this same night one summer ago, *I will tell—*

THE THREAD

FLOR SAYS, *OUR TIME is running out.*

We are through the veil in Neverland and we crowd close in the dark. The electric fan swings its face from side to side, but still the sweat gathers and trickles down our backs. There is Nisreen with her knees drawn up to her chin; Flor with her arms wrapping them together. There is Rose, cross-legged on my bed with a book of poems open before her.

There are small circles on the page, warped and wet.

Rose says, *He killed her on this night last summer, and this summer he's reg com final make. It isn't fair, and it isn't right, and there's nothing we can do.*

Flor breathes in all the still heavy air and says, *It's in our hands.*

And Rose shakes her head so sharp a curl slips loose and falls across her cheek. She says, *If we knew—if only she'd told us—*

I am here in the room with them. I am here, I swear it, even as I feel the tree against my back; even as the last light fades through the leaves. They are not real. They cannot be.

Flor says, *We've abandoned her.*

Rose says, *Don't say that. We're us four forever.*

And Flor says, *If we do nothing, we've abandoned her.*

The silence hangs like cobwebs. Before me there is the shimmer of stars, and the glare of the spotlights from the Naval Building, and one single code-flag flying: blue on white, *Xray*. Alone it tells us to stop all we have begun; to watch for new flags and their orders. And I seize with pain, because Flor is right: I abandoned them last summer, and this summer again on the First-Class Sail when I ran for the boy I could not kill. *Because they were not real*, I thought, as though that boy were any less a dream.

Nisreen says, in the quiet dark of Neverland: *We always say we're so shut away here that we don't know what's happening out beyond.*

She says, *Did you ever think of how it's true the other way, too?*

A wind draws itself up to where I sit and scatters leaves from the branches; from the vines that bind me close.

Rose says, beside me on the bed, *What do you mean?*

I have gone mad at last. I have given myself to the fever-dream that is eating me away. And perhaps I have not changed at all: still I am a little Butterfly staring up into the sky, and still I dream, and still I cling to hope from down in the dark of my grave.

Nisreen says, *I mean—the world could end, and we would keep lining up and marching to the mess—*

I slip free of the vines. The branches scrape along my skin and I bleed and do not care.

Nisreen says, *We're our real selves here and nowhere else.*

I am climbing down from my high perch, and the wind is pulling closer, and up beyond the branches all the stars die one by one.

Nisreen says, close enough to touch, *But what happens here will never leak out there into the world.*

And Rose says, *Good. It isn't theirs to know.*

I have found the forest floor. I walk the woodland trail where we marched one by one as Butterflies; as Dragonflies; as girls.

And Nisreen says, *I only mean—they'll never understand. No one will know the truth, no one but us.*

I have come to the end of the trail. Before me there is the great quiet of Lake Nanweshmot, and the masts of the *H.H. Bedford,* and that point on the shore where lovers kiss: that place that hides the lakeshore path where it curves home to Neverland.

Flor says, *Bound with our sisters 'til the grave.*

They are there tonight, beyond the veil. We are here and I will find us again.

I am a mad girl and my hour has come.

THE NIGHT

I DO NOT HIDE. I do not need to hide. They think I am dead.

I walk out of the woods. It is strange to be out of the trees and I stretch my arms wide and feel myself grow taller. There is a breeze stirring, electric, and a storm will come in soon.

The lakeflies and moths, the mayflies that should be dead: they leave their circles of light as I cross beneath them on the lakeshore path. They swarm and trail behind me, a veil and a gown. And there are fireflies, too, alighting on my hair. Lightning flickers high up in the clouds.

I AM MARGARET MOORE

My girls have faded away again. I am foolish to think they are real but I know it with all my heart: it is all I can believe. Flor said—summers and summers ago, forever ago I think—*It's only summer camp. It's not real.*

And Nisreen said, *It's the realest thing there is.*

It is true. We are all that is real.

I have betrayed us once and then again and they would be right to leave me, and I am sure they have been sent away, but still despite it they are here beyond me.

They are the hope that gleams far off. They are all I am not.

Not a single soul is out tonight. Only a dead soulless girl who has starved in the woods for—hours, days, decades; I cannot tell at all. I have left behind the parts of me I did not need, the parts that made me soft and theirs, that made me sit silent while they brought out knives and carved me apart and wrapped me in newspaper and twine.

I am all my own.

The wind blows hotter and higher, and it makes me dizzy, but not in that wilting way I was last summer. Instead I am dizzy with the power of it; with the past rushing up and back; with the enchantment of this night when I will find us here again.

Ahead of me there is Neverland. It is dark and the wood is more worn than it should be, but it is perfect and home. The sycamore stands strong beside it, with its leaves the dark green of this deepest night of summer. I walk up the path with my kingdom of flying things.

The door is open.

No: the door is gone.

The entrance to Neverland gapes and sneers with its teeth rotted out. There is not even the light up in the crook of the eaves, shining down to where the pavement disappears into our grotto.

I think: but I was just *here*; I was just here.

The wind gusts sudden and hot and laced with sulfur. There is a scattering of raindrops, or acid, or gasoline.

I run into Neverland. The dark inside is blacker than black; it swallows light and sound. I am flying up the stairs and outside there is a rasping flicker of lightning. And it is a storm. It is a storm the way it was last summer on this very same night.

I am here at the top of the stairs at last.

Our Marshall M is gone.

I find where it has always been. The paint is gray from summers on summers of hands slapping across it, for luck and for tradition. But a bright clean M burns into it, as fresh as it was when they built this secret home at the edge of the woods.

I hold my hand against that unsullied place; against the deep nail-hole.

We were here. We are here still.

The lounge is empty and strewn with old papers. All down the hall, with every twisting step I take, there is more abandon. Every door hangs ajar. Every window is open. There is no light but the far-off lightning, and there is no sound but the rising cry of the wind as it howls through the windows and across the hall and back out into the night.

They have taken us.

I draw a breath that rakes across my dry and scaling throat.

I scream and it is like nothing I have heard in all my life. It is the shattering of glass; the breaking of bone; the end of silence.

The wind shrieks back. The building shudders and the doors crash and crash in a row: on the lakeside they slam shut, and to the north they fly open. The cracks on the wall spread and grow. And I am bracing against the crumbling walls and dragging myself down the hall, and every room is gutted and empty.

The storm howls and howls and I think Neverland will fall to ruin with me here inside. With all of us—because we are still here, in the bones of this building, in the scars on the floor and that ghost of our Marshall M. I am looking past the wide-swung door into the room where my girls should be; where they are circled on the beds. But there is nothing here at all: only a broken window with its screen twitching mad in the wind, and on the floor in paint like blood three words that say:

GOODBYE MARGARET MOORE

I stagger back into the hall

and the doors hang wide like lidless eyes

and the storm comes hungry from the west

and the summers crash together now and crush me close between them.

In the lounge there is only the rush of the wind and the spinning of words on the floor. The old pages slip underfoot. And I stumble; I fall; and before me a page hovers yellow and stained and it says:

Let us go in together
And still your fingers on your lips, I pray
The time is out of joint—

When I blink the ruin falls back in taunting snapshots: Neverland is whole and loved, and we sleep fast behind closed doors, and the Victory Race is so very soon I taste it in the ether. The semaphores are bound up neat; there is our well-worn code-flags book; there are the heavy cinder-blocks. An old sheet hangs with painted words: OUR VEINS BLEED ORANGE, OUR HEARTS ARE GOLD.

I cry out in the dark for my sisters. I shriek with my

hands bleeding into the words on the floor: *Deck Five—Deck Five—*

I am flickering between the real and the wrong, this summer where my girls huddle beyond the veil and this summer with Neverland alive and dying, and last summer last summer last summer where I stand on the cusp of life and death and say to the boy who will kill me, *I will tell*, and say to the girls who have always been mine, *I am not yours—*

THE THRESHOLD

IT IS SECOND-CLASS SUMMER again and the phone rings and rings

and I am here with my hands pressed over my ears

and Nisreen says, *Mar, tell me what's wrong*

and down the hall a door bangs open and the ringing stops and a third classman says loud and finished, *Hello, this is Deck Five*, and then, louder: *Mar! It's for you.*

I sit up in my bed. Nisreen sits up, too, with her blanket around her, and she says, *Mar. Please.*

I want so much to tell her that I think I will be sick.

Nisreen says, *Tell us, we can fix it*, but she is wrong: I am in so drowning deep that all of us together cannot bring me up again.

I say—

Nothing.

I say nothing.

The door rattles and Rose says, through it, *Mar. Nisreen. Do you—*

And Flor cuts in and says, *We're coming in.* They do and the wind rushes in through the window and breathes Neverland alive.

Rose says, *They're calling for you, Mar.*

And Flor stands with the storm biting at her neck and she says: *Whatever you need us to do, we'll do it.*

I go to my wardrobe and stare into the mirror. I am a girl's face and a girl's fine flax-blond hair. I am soft enough to ruin.

I say, *I am not yours anymore.*

Flor says, *Yes you are, you stupid girl. You'll always be ours.*

And Rose says, *Mar. Tomorrow is the Victory Race, and we'll win together and storm the lake and sing our Deck Five hymn—*

He has taken this too. He has taken the Victory Race from me. It is a thing the world outside will never understand, and last week it burned a hole in my chest: it was everything.

Tonight it is nothing at all.

I say, *I'm sorry. I'm sorry—*

Outside the wind moans. The leaves of our sycamore rush and fight.

I say, *They're coming to take me away.*

It will be my parents on the phone, and they will tell me to bring my things and come out to meet them at the gates. They are coming for me and I am already gone.

I am walking, alone, out to where the phone hangs swaying.

I am listening, alone, to the crackling of static through the storm.

I am breaking, alone, when my mother says: *Margaret, it's time to go.*

I cannot. I will not.

I am dropping the phone and I run for the stairs, and my hand flashes up to our gold Marshall M and for one broken second I stop and am still: I am a mayfly in amber.

My father said, once, *This day is endless, too.*

And no matter how many new summers pass by I will stand at this threshold, in boat shorts and grief, with my name on my heart. I am here and my own, and not stolen away from this sacred safe-harbor where I am a girl.

My mother said, once, *Promise me you'll be my little summer-girl always.*

Tonight that summer-girl is gone and they have made it so.

Tonight I cling to our gold M
Tonight I let it go—

THE WAKING

THERE IS BLOOD ON the floor and it says:

GOODBYE MARGARET MOORE

There are pages spotted with mold and rain and they say:

Let us go in together
And still your fingers on your lips, I pray

They did not leave me last summer: I left them, and I left myself, and tonight all the world is splintering away and I will be lost if we do not come for her in the lashing rage of the storm—

I am digging out from my grave. I hit my palm against the wall, against our seared-white Marshall M, and leave it streaked with blood.

There are words on the floor and they say

The time is out of joint—

Behind me a door slams open and closed, and Flor shouts, *Deck Five, get up, get up.* There is a pounding at one door and another and the clang of the reveille bell. We are shaking our roommates to life and the words race breathless across our lips: *Mar is gone.*

They have come for me—

THE DECK

I REMEMBER THE STORM.

I remember the flicker of lightning and the roll of thunder.

I remember the shouts and the swinging beams of flashlights. Girls running out into the wind; into the rain. Nisreen in her long white nightgown. Flor in a robe and her saddle-shoes. Rose in a silk pajama shirt with her boat shorts, barefoot, blasting away on the old metal whistle she kept from our Butterfly days.

They are running, we are running past the girl who died by lightning, and she is lit up again: her clear impassive face; her outstretched hand; that butterfly on her fingertips with its fire-orange wings dead gray. We are flying across the drill-field and it shudders under our feet. And if there were ever a night when the field would crack open and swallow us into that hollow beneath, it would be tonight.

Tonight all the dark underneath is out and singing through the air. Singing up and down our arms, singing through our feet. We are bleeding into the grass and it is not that we cannot feel the pain: it is that we do not give one single damn. We are shouting. We are screaming. We are running for the water. And they are coming for us: the ensigns and the lieutenants; the director; the man who lives in that grand old Victorian on the west shore.

We will not let them have us.

One of us falls. One of us pulls her up.

Flor shouts:

We are—

We shout:

Deck Five!

We are running for the boats. We are running for the racks where they keep the sails and the rudders and the oars. The sky is on fire, and all the world is dark and light, and Lake Nanweshmot is furious and foaming.

We are running for the boats. We are running for the shore.

We are running dead into the storm.

I AM MARGARET MOORE

THE DARKNESS

THIS TIME I DO not go to the lakeshore. I dig deep into the heart of Marshall instead, across the quads and beneath the tree where I watched that trapped flying thing die all those weeks ago. It is dark here, wrapped in the rise of ivied buildings, and almost before I can think I have run through a propped-wide door and into warmth and light.

I am in the Hall of Honor. The lights blaze even so long past taps and there is a buzzing blue to them. I should not be in this spoiled place.

I look back.

Outside the wind rushes and there is a great crash and a branch plunges to the ground. It is far around to the road, and farther still back to the Admiral's Walk, and I am racing time itself.

It is only a door. It is only a hall.

I run into the light.

It is wrong: I know it right away. It has the cold glare of hospital rooms, and the air tastes like blood and metal, and there is something more, and worse.

I fly past tall cases of trophies and basketball nets. The Hall is longer than I remember, or shorter: I cannot tell. They have crowded the photographs too close. Class after class, and all in white and plaid, and all with the horsemanship building rising up behind, its brick turrets a fortress against white skies.

We are here, our third-class summer. But we are not second-to-last the way we should be. They have hung more portraits, crowding above and below and beside, and when finally I slow to make sense of it, I cannot find us at all. A thousand blank-eyed strangers stare and stare.

Something is not right and if I look any longer I will turn us to stone. I have already, I think. I have frozen all these faces on the wall, and turned them dead and timeless.

I should not have come this way.

Ahead there is the turn to the door, and I cut gasping and frantic out into the dark. Then I am in the storm again, in front of the chapel and past the infirmary; across the parade field; and then at last I am on the road and caught up in the tunnel of trees. Far off through the branches there is the faintest glow of the lights on each Butterfly cabin, and we are safe in our beds, drifting off to blissful sleep.

I am not a Butterfly anymore. I am a dull gray moth with sharp teeth and downy wings. I am a dead ghost girl beneath the floorboards and it is the very last night of our very last summer. Our time is almost up. I will find myself tonight, and I will lead them through the storm to the place where I cannot rest, and I will tell—

I AM MARGARET MOORE

THE CONDEMNED

THE DRIVE TO SHADY BLUFF is choked with vines.

Here the leaves grow so close even this storm cannot quite reach; here the driving rain is a muted drizzle; here the lightning is far off and toothless.

It is there ahead of me, crowned in sycamores. Where the trees open up I see it, white and wood and dressed in vines. When the lightning flashes it turns the wash of rain to a million shards of light; into a glow that lingers long after the thunder.

I stand at the edge of the woods; at the end of the world. It is very dark.

I stand in the rain on the lawn: on what was the lawn once before I turned it to stone.

I am walking across the lawn. The grass licks high around my knees. It has grown much too fast—faster than it should in these bruised weeks. But here there is no time: here there is only one long unbroken summer, stretching on and on.

I am four years old and stepping backward off the pier.

I am sixteen and diving naked into the shallows.

I am eighty and sitting in the shade with an ugly bright blanket blooming from my hands.

I am dead and I am walking to the kitchen door; up three steps to the little stoop. The paint is peeling and there is a plank nailed across the door with a sign pinned to it and it says:

DANGER. CONDEMNED.

There is a plank nailed across the door but above it the window is broken. The rain and the wind climb through and I follow them. Glass rips at my hands; at my leg that drags behind me when I lurch through the broken place, and I think: good. My blood is in this place already.

The floor is damp and littered with leaves. The kitchen table is where it has always been and the chairs have toppled, and there on the floor—a pile of blankets.

I crouch down and clutch at them.

We were here. Only weeks ago, we were here, and tonight the blankets reek of mold and death. There are creatures living in this house. The lake and the woods are claiming back what once was theirs.

It is not real. It is a fever-dream and it is my grief and the secrets I have kept, and they are threading me with poison so I will give myself to them; so I will let the silence push me down into the mud and nail the floorboards fast above my bones.

I stand up. I go to the door and look into the living room and it is a cavern with the same blown leaves and damp. Mold climbs the walls. They have let this place run to ruin and I am furious; I am heartsick; I do not understand. The books are scattered on the floor. A dozen photographs have fallen with their glass shattered away. When I look down my own face stares up at me.

She is here and she is waiting. I follow her out to the porch.

In the blind dark my grave is darker still: unvisited since I pried the floorboards up. I fall to my knees on dead leaves from summer turned to fall: leaves swept in and left to crumble on wood that once shone bright. Down in the dark there is not even the gold gleam of my name. There is only the white of bones half-buried in the dead wings of mayflies. And I think: *Ephemeroptera.* They have lived their whole lives here on Lake Nanweshmot, blooming and flying and dying unnoticed, and soon they will be dust.

Here time has gathered high.

Here I am dying on the floor. I am only pain and growing spots of gray and I want to go out to the shore and scream for my girls. They will come for me and I will tell them the truth, and they will forgive me and it will not matter that I am dying; we will be us girls again, and the truth will live in them.

I say, *I'm going to tell them—I'm going to tell—*

He says, *no, you won't.*

I see him only in glimpses now. I think there are mayflies in my eyes. I think I will say to him, *I will write words,* but there are moths in my mouth, there is blood in my throat, and I am far above myself. He is prying up the floorboards. He is digging my grave and I am dead and in the glow of the lantern the moths dance, and their wings are dipped in blood.

I am alone at my grave.

I cannot look any longer at the place where he threw me away. I am crawling out into the broken starlight and shattered glass. And I think: all is lost. I am alone and mad, and no one has come to find me, and soon I will be not even dust and bones: soon I will be nothing at all.

And I think: I loved a boy once, before all this.

I think: It is summer. It is always summer.

I think: Margaret, it's time to go.

She is here and I have her again and I think: perhaps it is enough.

She is here and she is smiling at me, smiling up from the floor. She is only an old photograph, slashed with glass and faded to the pure stark white of bones.

She is faded from sunlight and warped from rain but she is smiling bright with her Butterfly sash over her shoulder; with her arms flung around her girls. Behind her there is the little porch with its twin flags: forty-eight stars and thirteen stripes and one Marshall M, ours always.

She is faded to white and gray, this little summer-girl. But still she stands bound with her sisters 'til the grave: still she wears her name over her heart.

I say, and in the silence there is no one to tell me I cannot speak: *I am Margaret Moore.*

I say, and when I am all alone there is no one to tell me I am nothing: *I am a Marshall girl, a Deck Five girl. I am a little summer-girl. I am a girl who loved a boy. I am a girl who has made a choice and I am not ashamed.*

And I think: it does not matter after all, what he told me.

I am a Butterfly gazing up at the flyby and I am a Deck Five girl lying starry-eyed in the dark on the *H.H. Bedford* and I am a girl who got herself in trouble and it does not matter. It does not matter.

I am Margaret Moore.

I have died, but I have lived. I have been a girl: a fleeting fragile thing. I have been a girl: eternal, eternal, eternal.

It is enough, I think.

THE BALLAD

I STAND IN THE rain on the shore of Lake Nanweshmot.

Behind me the sycamores are overgrown and the sunporch is shuttered forever. A very long time has passed. I am a dead girl in the shadow of a dead house and all around me is the driving rain and the waves.

I am alone.

I am floating and fading and I think: I could walk into the lake and let the clear black swallow me down.

I could leave this place the way I did not when he killed me.

I crouch down on the shore. The waves roll in again and again and there is foam lined on the rocks. I run my hands along the smooth of clam-shells; the ridged spirals of long pointed shells; the whorl of little snails.

I step into the water. It is cold and sharp and I cannot believe I am not real. I close my eyes and in the gray he sits beside me, cast in light and shade, and watching as I die.

The waves tangle at my feet. The vines have pulled me down to where the truth waits.

He watches and does not speak.

I say, and it is slashed through with pain: *something is wrong—*

He watches and does not speak. All is orange light and gray shadow; storm outside and still within.

I say, and the words spill blood: *I think I am dying.*

He says, *You are already dead.*

And I think: he knew that I would die. He wanted me to die.

I say, and it is torture: *Why—why—*

I cannot say more. And I think: he has taken my words.

He says, *You were going to tell.*

There are mayflies; there is a whole swarm covering me. I feel the beat of their wings and the weightless weight of their feet.

Ephemeroptera, I think, and it is words that have made and unmade me.

I say, but I do not say:

To foe of His - I'm deadly foe -
None stir the second time -

There is light and there is dark. I cannot remember the rest.

But I am not there on the floor. I am in the lake with water swirling at my ankles. Above me the rain gathers light from the dark.

I am not a thing to be thrown away.

From where I stand, Marshall is only a dark stretch of shoreline and the lamps on the lakeshore path; the gleam in the steeple.

I have not finished what has kept me in this place.

Tonight I am only frail thin wings and a life meant to be over, but it is mine: I alone will decide what becomes of me.

I stretch my arms wide and I drink in the sky and the storm. And I say:

To foe of His - I'm deadly foe -
None stir the second time -
On whom I lay a Yellow Eye -
Or an emphatic Thumb -

I know what I must do.

THE GREEN

I WILL NOT COME back to Shady Bluff.

When I walk out of the lake I gaze at this holy place for the last time. At the sign with its letters peeling away; at the shuttered sunporch. At the rain streaming down the white wood.

I say to the girl with blood in her throat: *We are alive.*

I am dead beneath the floorboards but I am walking away.

I am in the overgrowth of the drive.

I am on the road.

I am in the woods, slipping sure-footed among the trees. This forest and this lake have let me live with them and bide my time until I could understand this strange spotted summer; this dream I have lived since that night in the storm.

I am before the Naval Building. The lights shine and shine on one code-flag, blue on white. *Xray: Stop all you have begun. Await my signal.*

On the lawn there are shouts and screams; there are lights swinging broad. They are on the green and they are on the shore. Flor grasps at a wherry and drags it onto the beach. The waves are wild and terrible.

Nisreen says, *We'll die if we go after her.*

Flor says, *She'll die if we don't.*

But the storm lashes hard and lights glare all around and a lieutenant shouts through a megaphone: *Deck Five, stop where you are.*

Lightning shoots down and ignites the lake and for a splintering instant all the world is aflame.

They have us surrounded. There are too many of them. They grab our arms and unlock the Naval Building. They push us inside.

The lights have all gone out.

We are in the dark. We are in our nightgowns and our robes; we are barefoot and in saddle-shoes. We are caged and we are breaking.

Rose says:

Margaret Moore. Find Margaret Moore.

And we say her name, all of us:

Margaret Moore!

Searchlights sweep across the lake. Across the fleet, straining at their lines; across the *H.H. Bedford* at her mooring. We are a storm of girls trapped here on the shore, and one of us is out in the night in a boat that will break.

And we are saying her name in one voice:

Margaret Moore!

It is an echo still as I stand on the path. The wind has calmed but the rain pours down and I can feel them here.

I climb the stairs up to the roof of the Naval Building. There is change here and I do not understand it—how the windows are an unfamiliar shape; how the gold-plated list of regatta winners has too many rows of names. There is a plaque just inside the door that says, THE WINSTON-BEDFORD NAVAL BUILDING, RECHRISTENED HOMECOMING 2002. In the photograph below it a white-haired lovely woman, laughing, breaks a bottle of champagne against the balcony. The colors are strange and sharp.

There is something familiar in her eyes; something that makes me want to cry.

I cannot stop to think of what it means. I am afraid I already know.

And I am climbing up and up and I am here on the roof in the rain.

They are in Neverland tonight. It is ruined and empty,

but it is locked safe against the storm and we are tucked beneath our blankets. All of us but three—all of us but four.

Flor has watched the shadow that crossed back to Neverland those purple-gray dawns when she woke early to raise the flag.

Nisreen has seen those nights when I was sick.

Rose has said his name.

A summer ago they had us wet and caged when dawn broke through. There were boats on the water; men searching when the reveille cannon sounded.

They sent us home to Neverland.

We marched back down the lakeshore path together. Barefoot and in saddle-shoes. In nightgowns and our boat shorts. We sang our deck hymn loud enough that everyone at Marshall, everyone on Lake Nanweshmot, everyone in all the world could hear our cry: *Forevermore we are Deck Five.*

A summer ago a wherry washed up in pieces on the shore. Margaret Moore's parents stood stunned at the gates and the director stood with them, and the chairman of the board, that VanLandingham man, and they told them Margaret was dead out on the lake.

They did not hold the Victory Race. They sent us away, unwhole. They told us we knew nothing and they meant we knew too much.

A summer ago the storm raged but tonight all is still.

Nisreen and Flor lie wrapped together, and soon they will go home alone, but tonight even Lieutenant Caldwell at the door could not tear them away from each other. Rose sits on my bed with a poetry book in her hands.

I am caught here beyond the veil, but tonight it will not matter: we are us four forever.

Nisreen stirs and Flor says, *What is it?*

Nisreen says, *Mar.*

She is rising and standing at the window.

Outside there is a mayfly on the screen. And then another, and another, and another, until the screen is all coated in wings and thin translucent bodies.

Nisreen says, *We have to go back.*

I have come to the roof of the Naval Building. At my feet is the metal box that holds the code-flags and the lid is so heavy—so heavy for my hands that do not know how to grasp, and it drains all my strength from me.

I steel myself against the pain. I throw the lid open. And everything spots gray and orange and I see them, far away and through the veil, stealing out onto the lawn. They are on the lakeshore path and there is a dancing tangling swarm of mayflies pulling ahead of them; pulling through the dead still of the night.

Rose says, *Look.*

I am in the driving rain. The wind has risen up again, and stronger than before, and I think it is because of me. I am dragging every drop of strength from my dead fingers; I am fastening flags together, and I think: *I will write words.*

I clip the first three flags to the line and hoist them. It tears through me with the same pain as the poison did that night at Shady Bluff.

There is no one out in the rain. No one, not even me, because I am already dead. And yet they are here: I know it.

This moment is eternal and so are we.

I am in the driving rain, and they are in the calm. Ahead of them the swarm of mayflies breaks apart. Ahead of them three flags climb the mast on the roof of the Naval Building. Their night is dead calm, but the flags fight and snap in the wind:

Mike, Alfa, Romeo.

Rose says, *Mar.*

Flor says, *It can't be.*

Nisreen says, *It is.*

I clip three more flags to the line and let the ensign's lone *Xray* fall at my feet. I am fading and I do not know how long I will last; I do not know if they will understand. The rain is so cold on my skin that I think it is not summer at all. I pull at the line and it is too heavy, and there is blood under my nails, and the pain from that night is back and it wrenches the air from me.

Juliet, Victor, Lima.

Jack VanLandingham.

I can hear them, I think: last summer, screaming on the lawn. And this summer, silent on the lakeshore path, and there are fireflies above them. Everything is beginning to move very fast; to shiver between here and there; between then and now, and I think: *The time is out of joint.*

I pull at the line and it will not move. I lean with all my nothing-weight and still it does not move. The rope digs into my hands and bright blood rushes out and soaks into the line but does not stain it, and still it does not move. And I am in the watercolor, I am on my back in the mud, I am glass-eyed on the floor of Shady Bluff.

I pull and I scream and at last the rope begins to drag down. I cannot see them now; I can see only the driving rain and not their clear still night. I can see only the growing spots of gray. I do not know if they have understood, or if they will believe this impossible thing: that I am gone and I am here.

I am so very very tired, and with every inch I move the line I slip deeper into the gray, the way I slipped when I pushed that boy into the water and tried to drown him—

and I see his face there

and I feel a great strength curling up from the deepest place in the lake

and I scream and I scream and the line begins to move.

I am almost out of time.

My hands shiver paler and I can almost see that they are not there: like a mayfly before a light. I can almost feel that deep dark swallowing me down. But I am unclipping the flags and digging for three more, and there is so much I want to say, so much I need to say, and I am sliding toward a long vast darkness.

I am dying.

I clip three flags together. I hoist them with a pain that rips down my spine and explodes in my skull; in my chest; in my belly where that monster tried to make its home. They crawl up and I am leaning with all my weight, and my skin is ripping away, and I am floating and fading and I do not know if they will understand and I do not know if I have raised them high enough and I fall

and I fall.

I have fallen to the flat of the roof. The rain pours down and down and it is coursing across my skin. It is scattering into my eyes. It is dancing across the concrete.

I think I have failed.

I cannot stand. I am bleeding: from my hands where I raised the flags; from everywhere, the way it happened when the boy who said he would save me killed me instead.

I think: *I am sorry.*

Then there is lightning above me

and through it all the rain glows and glows

and my head begins to fall
and I see it above me for one glorious hopeful second:
three flags fly proud in the storm.
Golf, November, Three.
I have done it.
It is summer and we are here together on the lake
and I am floating
and I am floating
and it is only gray and rain
and my eyes turn to glass
and I am gone.

THE LIFETIME

I AM A LITTLE summer-girl: a naiad. I live in a holy perfect house on the shore of Lake Nanweshmot. All summer I wake with the sun and I swim in the bright clear blue and I float in the dappling shade. My father is a wise measured man who smokes cigars and reads everything; who gives me books full of gods and men; who tells me I am immortal. My mother stacks my nightstand high with fairytales and poetry; with love-stories and Audubon prints. My grandmother kisses my hair and wraps me in blankets and tells me stories and I forget she is not still a girl, my age. At night when the light is still in the sky I fall asleep, spent and sunburned, and outside my windows the crickets chirp and the mayflies hover weightless.

I am a little summer-girl: a naiad. For six weeks every summer I live in a cabin in the woods with eleven other girls, and at night we sit in a circle around the campfire and we sing, *push onward and conquer and never say fail.* High up in the trees the fireflies roost in branches with their tails glowing bright, and I do not want the summer to end; I do not want us to end. And when I look up into the stars, I think we will be here forever. We are beautiful; we are girls; we are summer and timeless; we are summer and fleeting.

I am a little summer-girl: a naiad. It is my third-class summer and there is a bright shining pin on my collar and a boy says, *Will you walk with me?* I say yes: why would I ever say anything else? And I am climbing brave and weak-winged out of the water to fly along the lakeshore path, and around me the fireflies dance, and everything is radiant. That night I begin to fall in love with a boy who is beautiful and bright.

I am a shining summer-girl: a subimago. It does not matter that it is not summer. It is always summer. I am in love and I gleam with the glory of it. It is romance and secrets; it is passion and shouting; it is dancing under the streetlamps. It is poetry I whisper into the stars and a heart waiting to be broken.

I am a shining summer-girl: a subimago. I am caught in the road with a bright fast car. I am dizzy and falling on the lakeshore path. I am saying *no no, there is no boy.* I am saying nothing at all with the stars above me and the mud below. I am a common whore and a disappointment. I am running out into the storm. I am orange and gray and buzzing.

I am a shining summer-girl: a subimago. I am a dead girl but I do not know it because here I am safe with my sisters; here there is no world beyond; here we are girls. I am bleeding dark secrets that I cannot understand but I will. I am the lakeflies swarming and the vines that pull a boy down to drown him, and I do not know why, but I know the truth: I am a loaded gun.

I am a dying summer-girl: an imago. I am nothing and I am dead and I am gone. I will not come back to this place; I cannot come back. But the truth is mine, and I will write words, and I am not afraid.

Above me there are stars and fireflies
and below there is the deep dark of the lake
and I am a loaded gun
and the gun goes off.

I AM MARGARET MOORE

THE GIRLS

WE ROW OUT ONTO the dead-still lake. We are silent. We are four.

It is our first-class summer, the night before the Victory Race. We have rowed out onto the water. We lie in wait.

We throw rocks at his window. Smiling up from the green, standing over that place where the earth is hollow.

We say, *Will you walk with me?*

He says, *Yes.*

Why would he ever say anything else?

We walk across the grass; we pass by the cannon. There was a girl there once, on her back in the mud with her eyes fixed on the stars. She is not there anymore.

We walk to the shore and push a wherry into the water.

He says, *We can't go out.*

We say, and we are smiling bright, and we are girls: *We won't get caught.*

We kiss him.

We are on the lake. It is smooth as a mirror; as mercury; as truth and lies. He asks where we are going and we say not to worry. We have the rudder-oar and he is only rowing. It is our choice where we will go.

Out on the water the *H.H. Bedford* stands silent at her

mooring. Every mast and spar gleams in the moonlight. She is silver and white; she is beckoning. She is a great tall ship trapped here on this lake, but tonight her sails will fill.

We are on the lake and we are gliding into the shadows beyond the ship. From here he cannot see the shore: he can see only the dark of the water and the faraway lights circling it in, glowing orange at every lakehouse. He should know better than to trust us; he should know better than to think his secrets are buried with the girl he killed last summer.

He does not.

We smile at him and he reaches for the life preservers hanging over the stern. He says, *Rose Winston, I never would've thought you'd take a boy out in the middle of the night. I thought you were a good girl.*

We say, *We are all good girls.*

He is laughing. He has forgotten all about the dead girl. Not because he did not love her: because he must. He will not think of the wind that rushed up when he shouted to his friend on the wherry; he will not think of the sunlit afternoon when he fell from the Island and she spoke into his ear.

She is dead, he thinks.

She is dead.

Tonight there is a girl watching him with a smile on

her face as he climbs up onto the ship. *We are all good girls*, she says, and he does not think to wonder what it means.

He says, *I wish summer never had to—*

The rope snaps.

He shouts.

He is falling.

It is not far but it is far enough. He is stunned and seeing stars. He says, and it is thick and gray, *what happened—*

We are all around him. We are leaping down from the deck with a pocket knife in our hands; with the Butterfly logo on the handle and frayed rope across the blade. We are pulling around from the port side in another wherry with a sail rolled up behind us; with rope bound in figure-eights; with the boat riding low in the water. We are catching his hands in ours.

He says, *what the hell*, and the place where he fell is damp with blood.

We are girls. We are stronger than he is when he tries to push us away: we are lashing the rope around his wrists and his ankles. He is shouting now and telling us he is hurt; that the joke is over.

We wait until he stops to gasp and catch his breath.

We say, *Did you think we would never come back for her?*

We are rowing away from the *H.H. Bedford.*

He is pleading; he is shouting; he is laughing. He does not know which story to choose. He does not know how to be anyone but what will serve what he wants.

When we are tired of his shouting we take an old crew sock and shove it deep into his mouth.

He is silent now. All is silent and all is still.

We row out and out in our two wherries. We do not speak. The night is so beautiful it makes us cry. It is the end of the summer.

For this last night, we are girls: we are us four forever.

There is no sign to mark the place where the water is the deepest, but we feel its pull even floating high up on the surface. Below us there are a thousand; many thousand gold nametags. We dropped ours from the *H.H. Bedford* on our First-Class Sail. Three gold pins through a sheet of paper torn from the Victory Race notebook, and on it, we wrote two words: *Margaret Moore.*

In our first wherry the boy strains and sweats. He cannot speak.

He cannot make a choice.

He fights us but together we are unconquerable. Together we wrap him close in a sail. We tie him tight with knots we learned when we were Butterflies; we tether him to the cinderblocks we have hauled back and forth all summer in the shadow of our gray wood home.

We do not grant him last rites. But we think of the words

from the book that was Mar's once, and then was ours, and now belongs to every Deck Five girl:

Though I than He - may longer live
He longer must - than I -
For I have but the power to kill,
Without - the power to die -

Together we lift him out of the wherry and let him fall against the silver; into the black.

He is sinking down. Twenty feet; fifty feet. Below him there are many thousand nametags waiting with their silent metal teeth; with their letters faded to immortality.

We do not know what his last words would be.

We do not know if he is sorry.

We do not wait for him to sink to the mud. We are already rowing away. Behind us the rippling of our oars smooths flat and the still waters keep our secrets.

We will never speak of this night again.

We will never forget.

The lake is dark and deep. The water is black and moonlit.

We walk home along the lakeshore path with fireflies in our hair.

HANNAH CAPIN

THE VICTORY

IN THE MORNING THE ensign on duty finds code-flags strewn across the roof. It was the storm: that is what he tells himself. But high on the mast three flags hang listless: *Golf, November, Three.*

Can you take off persons?

Everyone knows the story of the girl who died out in the storm; the girl who was lost on the lake. It has been five dozen summers since but she is not forgotten. The Deck Five girls who hold her secrets say she watched from this rooftop the night that boy disappeared, the summer after she died.

They say, *She drowned the boy who killed her.*

The ensign should not be afraid. They would laugh at him.

But he is afraid, because it is tradition. Everyone knows Margaret Moore has wandered this place since that night in the storm. She is the lights that flicker in the infirmary, and the gusts that knock the sailboats down, and the clanging of the carillon bells at the Gold Star Ceremony forty summers ago. She is the crack across one portrait in the Hall of Honor, no matter how many times they replace the glass across that dead boy's face: JACK VANLANDINGHAM, REGIMENTAL COMMANDER, FINAL MAKE, 1959. She is the footsteps on the stairs in Gambol Hall, long past taps. It is condemned now: they will tear it down next week. Everyone says, *Good riddance.* Everyone says, *That drowned girl haunts Gambol Hall.*

Everyone says it except Deck Five, and Deck Five does not call it Gambol Hall at all. Deck Five calls it Neverland, and they have left her room empty all these stacking summers. They have saved her place in the lineup and her seat in the mess.

The ensign takes down the flags. He leaves the mast empty: today there is the Victory Race, and they will hoist code-flags again and again. He says to the others, when he gives in and tells, *It's been sixty-three summers since she died out in the storm, and anyway, it's only a story.* But still he shows them the words she left: still they read her name.

It is the last day of summer. The sun is rising and it is very hot.

I am here.

I am not bound to the lake anymore; I am not bound to my scuffed saddle-shoes or my nametag. But I am watching still, from far off, and I am here.

When it is time for the Victory Race the decks march in, chanting loud. All the boys and the Lower Camp line up on the lakeshore path, and all the old Marshall regiment who have come back to watch again come in with them.

There is the blast of an air-horn.

There is a rush of sails. Out on the water it is Deck Five in the lead and a Winston girl at the helm. A Bedford by name, but a Winston by blood and in the way she sails. There is a gold number five pinned to the left side of her collar.

There is a gold pin on the right side, too. It is the Marshall M, almost, but looking closer it is written double.

Deck Five wears a double M for Margaret Moore.

It is a day beautiful and bright. Far off over the west shore stormclouds pile high but they will not reach us here. We are Deck Five, and we are running and we are rowing; we are filling a tall barrel with lakewater; we are waving semaphores. We shoot arrows and rifles; we read messages in code-flag hoists; and we run, we run, we run—

We have won.

We charge into the water. We are proud and bleeding; we are here in Lake Nanweshmot with our sisters; we are laughing and crying. We press our palms against our double-M pins for luck and for tradition.

The reg com calls the present arms and every hand comes up. A thousand salutes, from the Butterflies to the oldest men in the shade.

They play the Navy hymn. We sing our anthem.

I AM MARGARET MOORE

Deck Five the proud, Deck Five the bold
Our veins bleed orange, our hearts are gold

We are in the water, we Deck Five girls who have been swept out of Neverland; who have pried the gold M out of the wall and kept it ours. On our first night next summer we will say, the way we say each summer: *Every Deck Five girl at Marshall has touched this M. Margaret Moore has touched this M.*

We sing our Deck Five hymn.

We're staunch and true and bright and brave
Bound with our sisters 'til the grave

High up above I am watching. High up above we are watching, the four of us, from the Winston-Bedford Naval Building, rechristened nineteen summers ago by Rose Winston-Bedford. We are Rose with her son on the Marshall board; with her granddaughter sailing for Deck Five; with her lakehouse on the east shore and her numbers in the sky. We are Nisreen, living in Amman and New York City, still with her eyes on the horses she raises with her sons and her daughters: horses that run faster than the wind. We are Flor, who left Caracas when her husband died; who fifty years after our first-class summer moved to Brooklyn; who lives with Nisreen in a brownstone that beams with light and orchids.

We are Margaret, who writes words on the memory of every Deck Five girl. A poet and a dreamer and a girl who sees the good in everyone.

We are in the water with our arms around our sisters; we are on the roof of the Naval Building beneath dark glasses and gauze scarves. Last night I strung the flags up with the last of my strength: it is what I stayed here to do. Last night, sixty-two summers ago, they walked out into the calm and saw the flags.

The time is out of joint.

This day is endless, too.

We are Deck Five girls with our toes deep in the mud. We are on the beach, saluting: Butterfly girls who dream of the day it will be our turn. We are in the shade, old women with white hair, but Deck Five girls still for this eternal moment.

And we sing our hymn:

As Marshall girls we'll live and die
Forevermore we are Deck Five.

I have lived these five dozen summers in one. I have roamed the sovereign woods; I have become a wild mad girl; I have mourned for all we have lost.

I have made my choice: to stay for us; to redeem us.

and to write words

and to find the truth I already knew

and to find the boy who killed me

and to give him to the waters that have kept our secrets all these cobwebbed decades. To bury the boy who cut my shallow grave into the floor; to throw away the spotless boy who left me in the mud.

I have found us again: myself, and Rose and Flor and Nisreen, and all my Deck Five girls.

I am fading. I am floating above the deepest place in the lake, weightless and sunlit on the green green blue. I am drifting up with a breeze that could fill the tall ship's sails, and I am looking down at us there on the shore.

The woods are deep green. They grow wild by the place where Neverland stands empty and wilder still over Shady Bluff.

Lake Nanweshmot keeps our secrets.

I am plunging down off the dock, and I float free in the clear of the lake, and I look up and I am in the watercolor. All is bright sunlight; all is leaves and sky, and green and blue, and I am in love with it, and I am in love with us.

I am a little summer-girl.

I have used up the last of my time.

It is a very hot day: the last day of summer. The sky is

blue and the leaves are green and the water is cold and welcome.

And I am here, I am here, I am here—!

I am gone.

It is summer again and we are alive.

ACKNOWLEDGMENTS

My endless thanks to all who brought Margaret Moore into the light:

to Sarah Burnes, for understanding why I write

to Sara Goodman, for understanding what I write

to everyone at Wednesday Books and The Gernert Company, for your talent and passion and hard work

to Tori Bovalino and Kelsey Rodkey, for braving the very first read

to Liana and Cat and Katie and Jessica and Michelle and Kathryn, for all of it

to the Culver Haists, east shore and south, for aiding and abetting

to the Deck Five girls, forever

and most of all, to Lake Maxinkuckee, for each eternal summer.